DROW MAGIC

DROW MAGIC

CHRONICLES OF SHADOW BOURNE™ BOOK 4

MARTHA CARR

MICHAEL ANDERLE

DISRUPTIVE IMAGINATION®

THE DROW MAGIC TEAM

Thanks to our JIT Readers

Diane L. Smith
Dorothy Lloyd
Jeff Goode
Jan Hunnicutt

Editor

SkyFyre Editing Team

CHAPTER ONE

Claire Burton handed the oversized laminated menu to the waiter, and Ellis added a second item to the list of things she knew about her mother. One, she was a doctor, and two, she liked her eggs sunny side up.

The scope of what Ellis did *not* know about Claire loomed.

The server cleared her throat. "And for you, hon?"

Ellis hesitated, then replied, "Same for me. The number two egg plate, sunny side up."

She had waited decades for this reunion. Now, she searched for the perfect thing to say: the words that would bridge the distance. Her mind was blank.

Claire tapped her short, unpainted fingernails on the laminate tabletop. Ellis also kept her nails short, probably for different reasons. She doubted Claire made a habit of punching goons.

Then again, her mother had shot a guard in the neck without flinching. The man had been about to kill her. Claire's movements had been smooth and practiced.

Maybe her mother did more goon-punching than Ellis thought.

Tap-tap-tap went her mother's fingernails. "You're staring, Ellis."

Ellis wanted to hear Claire say her name a hundred more times. "So are you."

Claire surveyed the other patrons. It was mid-morning, and the diner was busy. Behind Ellis, a girl was babbling about horses between bites of pancake.

Claire pursed her lips. "Are you sure you want to eat? We need to talk to your father."

Her father. Ellis touched the half-moon insignia on the breast pocket of Claire's fatigues. "Dad told me that if I ever saw this symbol, I should run." She shivered.

Her mother frowned. "Are you warm enough?" The maternal concern made Ellis want to cry.

When they had emerged from the underground facility in the middle of Elysian Park, Ellis had turned her hospital gown into an approximation of a wrap dress, then stolen a sweatshirt from a yoga mom distracted by her kids' playground antics. She had no shoes, but the diner was busy enough that she had snuck in without anyone noticing.

"I'm warm," Ellis replied, "but I'm starving. Those pellets hardly qualify as food."

She shuddered again. The pellets had not tasted of anything, and they had reminded her of Flower's food.

The television in the corner grated on her nerves, but Ellis appreciated the white noise. Two perfectly coiffed anchors appeared on-screen and introduced their next story: Californian Senator Arden Chan was visiting Avenal State Prison to talk about overcrowding.

The video showed prisoners wearing light blue button-downs and navy pants in an enormous cafeteria. It was hard to see the food on the plastic trays, but it was not pellets.

Ellis' stomach grumbled. Claire's face pinched with regret, then flipped to neutral when she caught Ellis staring. The shift was so drastic and abrupt that Ellis flinched. "Right."

Claire stared over Ellis' shoulder at the girl of six or seven in the next booth, who was *highly* opinionated about the three flavors of syrup on offer. At that age, Ellis had been learning to pick locks with her grandmother while hiding from the other drow.

Ellis *was* hungry. Claire had informed her that she had been unconscious for a day and a half. Whether eggs would assuage the void in her gut was questionable. Landon and Percy were still down there. Percy's king cobra was too, although Ellis was too exhausted to muster much sympathy for a giant snake.

According to Claire, Landon was in the "intake lab." Ellis imagined cold metal tables and needles and shuddered again. The TV blared a political attack ad against Senator Chan. Apparently, since she was a Massachusetts native, she loved taxes.

Claire had switched from tapping her fingernails to clicking a ballpoint pen. The half-moon logo was printed on the side, along with the letters DRI.

"What does DRI stand for?" Ellis inquired. "Errol called you the 'moon men,' but that seems too casual." *Considering the people they murdered in cold blood.*

"The Dark Research Institute." Claire smiled sheepishly.

"It sounds sinister, but the phenomena we research are associated with darkness."

Ellis frowned. "There's nothing sinister about darkness. No one ever got second-degree burns from the moon."

Claire knew nothing about her daughter. The gap between the two women was widening.

Claire opened her mouth to reply, but the arrival of two steaming plates of food interrupted her.

Ellis was ravenous. She slathered a piece of toast with butter, then stuffed it into her mouth. The two eggs on the plate wobbled, and the undercooked egg whites made Ellis' stomach rebel.

Eventually, Claire noticed the two untouched yolky islands.

Ellis blushed. "I don't actually like them sunny side up."

Claire blinked in surprise. Then her eyebrows creased. "That's all right."

"I have questions."

Claire's face lit up, and her response was pointed and eager. "I'm sure your father will, too."

Ellis did not trust her mother's zeal. She wondered what Claire's face had looked like when she killed the guard. Self-defense notwithstanding, murder was a long way from "do no harm."

"Why do you work with them?" Ellis demanded. "They would have killed me."

Claire hesitated before replying. "I suppose you deserve an explanation. First, you should know that I haven't worked for the DRI for a long time, and the organization has changed. If I'd known what they'd become, I would have done something about it."

Heat bloomed in Ellis' cheeks, and she crossed her arms. "You're wearing a shirt with a DRI logo and holding a DRI pen. You said, 'When *we* found your blood.' What did that mean if you don't work with them now?"

The pen clattered onto the laminate. "I can explain! I left the DRI before you were born, but my DNA was still in their system."

Ellis narrowed her eyes. "Why did they have your DNA?"

"To check samples for cross-contamination in forensics work," Claire explained. "An old friend called me when your blood showed up on the wall in the police station."

"Which old friend?" Ellis challenged her. "The one who shot Charlie's boss? The one who killed the people at the commune in Topanga? The one who burned me with lightsilk?"

A man at the table beside them glanced over. His gaze caught on her bare feet, and he looked away. Hopefully, he would think Ellis was crazy and pay them no mind.

"You call it lightsilk? Not safesilk?"

"Nothing about that stuff is *safe*," Ellis retorted, although she knew that was not true. If her shadow magic powers had emerged as early as Rose and her friends had claimed, Ellis had probably spent a lot of her infancy wrapped in the fabric. "We use cave spider silk for... different things. How do you make the 'safesilk?'"

Claire's gaze showed her interest. She opened her mouth, then paused and reconsidered what she would say. "I haven't been around in a long time, so I'm not sure. Let's stay on track. Why was your blood on that police station's wall?"

Ellis swallowed. Thanks to her eidetic memory, she remembered the terror on Captain Jericho's face as though the incident had taken place yesterday. If he had collected a sample of her blood, he had been less frightened than she had thought. It had been funny at the time. It was less so now that he was dead.

"I was pretending to be a ghost."

Her mother snorted so loudly that their neighbor looked over again. This time, he frowned at Ellis' feet. Ellis hoped he would not complain to the staff and get them kicked out. She was not ready to go anywhere else with her mother.

Ellis waved their server over. She ordered more coffee, a stack of pancakes, and two slices of pie. If the pancakes were good, she might let her mother have some pie.

When the coffee arrived, she dumped cream into the mug and drained half the pot. "They don't have coffee at the homestead," she explained.

Claire snatched the cream from Ellis and doctored the other half of the coffee the same way. Another item on the list. "You deserve kudos for surviving to adulthood without killing anyone."

Ellis raised an eyebrow. "How do you know I haven't killed anyone?"

Claire's expression darkened. "I don't, but I want to know everything about you. The blood made me fear the worst. I thought I would never meet you, but here you are."

"Here I am," Ellis echoed. The camaraderie gave way to awkward silence. Then she blurted, "How did you meet Dad?"

Claire's gaze iced over before she smiled. "At a rave."

6

"What?"

"A *rave*." Claire repeated the word, amused. "I'm still not sure why he was there. I know so little about either of you."

Ellis knew the feeling. She would have to ask Connor about it later. *A rave? So embarrassing.* Ellis realized she had never been embarrassed by her parents before and blushed, but humiliation was better than tragedy.

"What were *you* doing at a rave?"

"Raving," Claire replied dryly.

Ellis found it hard to square the serious person across the table with her mental image of a raver.

"Some friends took me," Claire nonchalantly added.

"Rose?"

Claire's jaw dropped. "How do you know about Rose?"

"I tried to find you for a long time." Ellis did not want to cry. She shut her mouth and gestured for her mother to continue.

"I was with Rose," Claire confirmed. "She was a knockout."

"Still is."

Claire grinned. "That doesn't surprise me. I haven't seen her in years, which makes me feel terrible, but... circumstances intervened.

"Anyway, she dragged me to this horrible club in Hollywood back when it was grungy. Halfway through the evening, the DJ asks if there's a doctor in the building.

"They had this guy laid out on a merch table in the back. The merch girl wouldn't stop shouting about blood getting all over the T-shirts. I thought the guy was wearing a sheer purple shirt, but then I realized it was his skin."

"That was Dad."

Claire nodded. "He'd worn a full-head mask all night, and it was so dark in the venue his skin wasn't obvious unless you were up close. Which I was since someone had stabbed him."

Ellis gasped. She was unsure which was more shocking: that someone had stabbed her father or that her parents had met at a rave. "What did you do?"

"I packed the wound with gauze from a roadie's tiny first-aid kit. It was covered in merch stickers with band names like Sound Wound and Gland Guignol, but by some miracle, the contents were still sterile.

"The second the bleeding stopped, Con dumped a bottle of something over the bandages and pushed me away. However, I convinced him to let me bring him to my clinic to be sure. I don't think he needed medical attention at that point, but he was curious. There was a spark." Her smile was genuine, but her gaze was sad.

Ellis' father had never told her this story. Maybe he had not wanted Ellis to know that he had partied in Los Angeles. Surely, youthful indiscretions did not merit such an extreme response, but Connor Burton turned to stone when Ellis asked questions about her mother.

"What happened after that?"

"He came back. He'd appear in the night, and we'd drive around. The second time we met, I insisted on checking his wound. It had healed. I was working in a medical research facility, but I had just opened a small nonprofit clinic with a good friend, and we saw a lot of violent injuries. None healed that fast. I was stunned."

Ellis sighed. "I know what it's like downtown."

"I asked Connor if we could study his blood so we

could learn how he had healed so soon. When I learned how *old* he was, I realized it could revolutionize medicine. That was the start of the DRI."

Ellis' sympathy warred with suspicion. She had imagined her mother's clinic as a struggling noble enterprise, not the evil organization she had seen in the basement of the Bromeliad. "You started the DRI?"

"Yes, but I'm telling you, it used to be different. It's changed."

"No shit. If they hurt Landon..."

"They won't."

Ellis scowled. "They locked me in a cage and electrocuted me."

Claire's reply came after a pause. "They won't kill him. Drow are valuable to the DRI."

Her anger was a soft but steady pressure in Ellis' skull. "'Valuable?' Gold bars are valuable. Landon's a *person*."

"Yes, and he's almost certainly still alive." Claire sighed. "I'm so sorry, Ellis. I never meant for the Institute to turn out this way. I don't have the clearance to wander anymore, but the bits and pieces I saw were bad. An old friend tipped me off to your location, and I stole gear from a locker room and fibbed my way onto a guard team. I had to rescue you."

Ellis grimaced. "Dad won't talk about you. I had to build a network of informants to learn about you. It wasn't easy. They all want money."

Claire guiltily stared at her coffee. "I don't doubt it. Connor fought with my co-director at the clinic and disappeared before I could muster the courage to tell him I was pregnant. I had no way to contact him. I went to our meeting spot in the forest many times, but he never showed. After you were born and started showing your abilities, I tried again. He only opened the doors for you."

The lines on Claire's face deepened. Her frown lines were much deeper than the smile lines in the twenty-year-old photos Ellis had seen.

"Where have you been all this time?" Ellis finally asked. If Claire had been in Los Angeles, Ellis would have found her.

"Abroad."

Ellis sipped her coffee and tried to channel the patience Charlie Morrissey showed when interrogating suspects. *Is that what your mother is? A suspect?*

Claire's mouth tightened into a flat line. "It's a long story that we don't have time for, Ellis. Please. Your brother's life depends on me finding your father."

Dark undercurrents painted the word "brother." *I can't take Claire to the Swallow's Nest.* The realization felt like someone had scooped Ellis' insides out with a melon-baller.

Ellis had another option. If she put the locket on, her father could track her. He would only put on the matching ring if he suspected trouble, but he might already. Surely, someone in the homestead had realized that Landon was missing by now.

If the locket did not work, Ellis could leave her mother at her apartment and go to the homestead alone. The prospect made her uneasy, but she had few options.

Ellis put down her cutlery. "Let's go. I live nearby. Do you know where Min Da's Noodle Shop is?" The restaurant's menus proudly announced that the place had opened in the eighties.

Claire grinned. "That place is still around? Do they still make that mind-blowing *kalguksu?*"

Ellis grinned back. "It's my favorite."

Claire stopped Ellis from sliding out of the booth. "We haven't paid the check."

Ellis blinked and patted the pockets of her hospital gown. Claire did likewise with her fatigues.

"Shit," Ellis murmured.

Claire chortled. "How fast can you run?" she wryly asked. Then, she narrowed her eyes and repeated, more seriously, "How fast *can* you run?"

"Very fast." Ellis morosely stared at the remains of her pie. "I wish I hadn't eaten so much whipped cream."

CHAPTER TWO

Ellis winced as Claire pulled a shard of glass from her foot. The doctor's worried expression was more professional than maternal as she tore a strip off her shirt to bandage the wound.

"You ought to take a course of antibiotics. I forgot you weren't wearing shoes. Downtown LA isn't great for barefoot sprinting."

Ellis had an antibiotic mushroom ointment at home. Her feet ached from running on concrete, and the cut burned, but she had dealt with worse.

A couple of tears dripped onto the bandage as her mother tied it off, and Ellis frowned. "Are you all right?"

Claire wiped her eyes with her sleeve. "Fine. I missed so many years of tending to scrapes. I have a sudden urge to kiss it and make it all better."

Ellis' feet were the color of manure and smelled worse. She smirked. "Knock yourself out."

Claire stared at Ellis' foot, then met her daughter's gaze, and both women burst out laughing. The noise caused a passerby to peek into the alley, but they hastily moved on.

When they finished, Claire's eyes were brighter, although her cheeks were streaked with tears. She straightened and offered Ellis her hand. "Are you sure you can walk?"

Ellis accepted her mother's hand. Claire's skin was warm and smooth. "I'll be all right."

Sirens pierced the air as they approached the apartment building, and Ellis noticed a thick column of smoke dissipating into a low cloud. Ellis cursed and picked up her pace, then realized she had left her mother behind. Claire was limping, and it worsened the faster she walked.

Ellis hung back. "Are you okay?"

Claire winced. "Bad knees. We're not the dream team, are we?"

"Not at the moment."

They rounded the corner, and Ellis' heart rose into her throat. A fleet of emergency vehicles clustered outside her building. People streamed out the front doors, vastly outnumbering the geared-up firefighters.

Ellis scanned the building. Brown smoke emanated from a window beside the distinctive potted plants on her balcony.

Two nearby firefighters frowned at the smoke as their colleagues screwed a massive hose into a nearby hydrant.

"Think we'll put the blaze out?" one asked.

The other shook his head. "Maybe when pigs fly. This place is new construction, and that brown smoke was a flashover. Remember your training?"

Ellis did not listen to the rest of his sentence. She

sprinted for the lobby. The ache in her feet disappeared with the surge of adrenaline.

At the door, a firefighter blocked her path. *"Ma'am!"*

Ellis dropped her shoulder, barreled into the man, and burst through the door.

The alarm was a dozen times louder inside. It nearly stopped Ellis in her tracks, thanks to her sensitive drow hearing. She ripped pieces of cotton from her hospital gown and stuffed them in her ears, then pushed open the staircase door.

Ellis could not abandon Flower and the other animals. Percy would never forgive her. Adrenaline took her up the stairs. By the time she pushed open the door onto her floor, her muscles burned.

As Ellis approached her door, she realized she did not have her keys. Then she scoffed. *I'm Ellis-fucking-Burton. When did I ever need a key?*

Aggressive barking from inside the apartment pushed her doubts aside. Ellis drew two deep breaths, then slammed her heel into the door by the lock. She desperately hoped the loud *crack* was not a bone.

She then rammed her shoulder into the door, and the combination was enough. The weakened door burst open, and a cacophony of animal noises and miasma of smoke greeted her.

So did the barrel of a gun.

For a moment, Ellis thought it was her mother, but it was someone else in a DRI uniform with a gun in one hand and a plastic bottle in the other. Acrid kerosene assaulted Ellis' nose.

How had they found her apartment? Percy would never

have willingly told his captors where she lived. Maybe they had threatened to hurt the cobra.

Ellis' pulse slowed. She could handle this. She ate ordinary soldiers with human guns for breakfast, not that she had room after a stack of pancakes and a slice and a half of pie.

"Down on the ground with your hands above your head," the soldier barked. His fear undermined the command. "I have the MEC."

This second statement was not addressed to her. A comm crackled through the barking, chirping, and meowling.

Ellis spotted Flower. Her short, silver fur stood on end, and her ears were pressed to her head. Without hesitation, the dog pounced on the DRI soldier.

He instinctively turned toward the incoming canine rocket, and Ellis seized her chance. She drove her knee into the soldier's groin, then dug her fingers into his forearm and pushed his gun toward the ceiling. Two shots rang out.

She could not see the bullet holes through the smoke. She saw no flames in the kitchen or living room, but the smoke was thick and dark. Wherever it was, the fire was worsening.

Ellis twisted her hand. The soldier screamed and dropped the gun. Out of the corner of her eye, Ellis saw Flower carefully pick it up with her teeth and carry it away.

Ellis realized her fingertips were burning. The soldier's armor was covered in lightsilk. Ellis swore and wrestled the man into a chokehold. He scrabbled at her arm, but

Flower bit his foot to distract him. Seconds later, he slumped and went still.

Tears burned Ellis' eyes. She hauled open the front door, only to find the corridor choked with smoke.

Shit. She would not be able to coax the animals out through that. The balcony was her best chance of escape. The DRI had seized her grapnel when they captured her, but her old one was somewhere in here.

Ellis sprinted to her room with her arm over her face and flung open drawers while cursing her housekeeping. She found the gun buried in a pile of dirty laundry, from which she also grabbed a pair of jeans, a sports bra, and a T-shirt. She shoved her feet into the nearest pair of boots.

She jammed a pillowcase into the waistband of her jeans and wrapped another around her nose and mouth before returning to the living room. Sweat dripped down her back, and the smoke was now thick enough that she could not see all of Percy's animals. She could still hear them, which was good.

A long, furry creature emerged from the smoke, skittered up her leg, and wound around her neck. She reached up and scratched the ferret's belly. "Hello, Muffler."

Ellis slid open the glass balcony doors. The wave of fresh air was a welcome relief, and the menagerie streamed out to join her. Ellis caught a glimpse of the unconscious DRI soldier, sighed, and went back for him. She dragged him onto the balcony by his feet, then listened for stragglers. Hearing none, she slid the doors shut.

The firefighters were keeping the rubberneckers at a distance, but they saw her when she stepped out. They shouted and pointed, which prompted the firefighters to confer before two rushed to a truck.

Wormy alighted on the railing, eyed the assembled zoo, and squawked.

Ellis shooed the mangy pigeon away. "Get to safety!"

Wormy dodged her hand, then cooed and fluttered over to snatch a piebald guinea pig in her claws.

Ellis gasped, but the bird flew over the railing before Ellis could stop her. Wormy struggled, and the rodent squealed, but they steadily dropped until the pigeon deposited the guinea pig at a firefighter's feet. Ellis could not be certain, but she thought it was the man she had overheard. Ellis would have paid several gold bars to see his expression. *When pigs fly, huh?*

The particolored flock on the rail, consisting mostly of crows, squawked and cawed. The birds' feathers gleamed like oil slicks in the light filtering through the smoke. A scarlet macaw, a red-shouldered hawk, and a chickadee with its chest bravely puffed out joined them, and Wormy did too. The assemblage made space for the decrepit pigeon like she was a decorated war hero.

"Wormy, you're amazing."

The pigeon cooed, then pointed a wingtip at a mouse that was the size of a cornichon. The chickadee flapped over to grasp the rodent, and Ellis would swear that the mouse's jaw dropped in amazement as it was lifted into the air. *I'm flying, Jack! I'm flying!*

Ellis left the small creatures to the birds, although she narrowed her eyes at the hawk in warning when it clutched a reluctant rat in its talons.

The haze inside her apartment had thickened further and was now flickering with orange. Ellis had little time.

The firefighters had inflated an air cushion that was ten feet tall and made of bright yellow plastic on the sidewalk. Flower put her paws up on the rail and nervously eyed the cushion.

Ellis patted her head. "I wouldn't do that to you, girl." She eyed the unconscious DRI soldier. "You, on the other hand…."

She hauled the man over her shoulder, then tossed him over the rail, aiming for the cheerful red dot in the center of the cushion. He hit the bullseye and rolled to the side.

"Ten points!" Ellis exclaimed.

A short blonde woman pushed to the front of the crowd, and Ellis realized with a start that it was her mother. Claire brought her hand to her ear as the firefighters pulled the DRI soldier off the cushion, then looked up and saw Ellis.

Flower barked to draw Ellis' attention back to the task at hand.

The birds had cleared out the small animals. Next were the three cats: a rangy gray, an orange Persian with a face like a smashed pumpkin, and a small black cat Ellis had never seen before.

Ellis retrieved the pillowcase from her waistband and held it open. "It's this or jump," she informed them. The following violent unpleasantness cost her more blood than had the glass shard in her foot, but when it was over, she had a squirming sackful of cats.

She hooked the grapnel over the rail, then stepped over. Muffler squeaked and clawed her neck as he held on. The sack of cats, understanding that now was not the time to wiggle, had calmed.

Flower whined and backed away.

"Come on, girl," Ellis coaxed. "I promise I'll keep you safe."

Flower woofed, then vaulted onto the rail and into Ellis. The drow held on despite having the wind knocked out of her by the solid pit bull. The cats growled.

Flames licked the inside of the glass doors. They were out of time.

Ellis squeezed the grapnel's trigger, and the cable released with a whir, then lowered them to the ground. Ellis' feet touched asphalt, and Flower sprang off her chest. A firefighter rushed up to Ellis.

"Ma'am, are you all right—"

He was interrupted by the cats' emergence from the pillowcase. They had apparently decided they were fed up with this nonsense. The combined ball of gray, orange, and black fur scampered over his bunker gear, then separated and streaked into the crowd. Ellis could only imagine what the onlookers were getting with their phones.

Ellis also used the feline distraction to dart away. She threaded through the mob until someone grabbed her shoulder from behind. Ellis spun, prepared to strike, but relaxed when she saw her mother.

Claire's face was a humiliatingly familiar shade of red. *Now I know where I got it from.* Ellis barely had time to add that to her list of similarities before Claire shook her ferociously.

"What the hell were you *thinking?*" her mother hissed.

Flower's hackles rose, and she growled.

"Stop!" Ellis exclaimed, and the command worked on both woman and dog. Ellis caught a breath before noticing two firefighters pushing toward them through the crowd.

Ellis pulled Claire in the other direction. Flower would follow. "What happened to that soldier from the DRI?"

Claire grimaced in pain, but she kept up. "Two men dressed as paramedics took him away in a black van."

Ellis gritted her teeth. She hoped she would not regret saving the soldier's life. "They knew where I lived." It had taken her a while to piece together how, but she had managed in the end. *Damn you, Charlie Morrissey.*

Before she could follow this train of thought further, her right eye twitched, and she doubled over, coughing.

Claire touched Ellis' arm, which was scored with claw marks. "Are you all right? You're bleeding."

"I've had worse."

This was a lie. Ellis was injured, exhausted, and light-headed. Over the past twenty-four hours, she had been imprisoned, electrocuted, and stabbed in the foot. Her fingertips were burned, and her lungs and throat ached from the smoke. Landon had been kidnapped, Charlie had betrayed her, and Percy was a captive.

The world tilted. Claire caught her and lowered her to the ground. Ellis pressed her eyes shut as a coughing fit rattled her. She was certain she would find a lung on the pavement, but she saw nothing but black phlegm.

Ellis wiped her eyes and nose with the hem of her T-shirt. "I want to go home."

Claire frowned at the burning building, and Ellis shook her head and sniffled. As much as she had enjoyed life in the condo, it had never been home.

"Not there," she told her mother. "I wanna go *home*."

She wanted her little room full of bioluminescent mushrooms. She wanted to walk barefoot in the mushroom fields and feel her father's cool, calm hands on her forehead.

"You need medical treatment for smoke inhalation first," Claire argued.

Ellis shook her head. "Dad will know what to do." The drow had lived in unventilated caves for centuries. They were no strangers to lung disease.

"Are you sure?" When Ellis nodded, an emotion Ellis did not recognize passed over her mother's face. She was too exhausted to work it out. "All right. Let's find your father."

CHAPTER THREE

With nothing to distract him—no phone, TV, books, or even the back of a shampoo bottle—Charlie Morrissey had plenty of time to consider the betrayal on Ellis' face when he had turned his gun on her. He had hoped switching sides would have given him credibility with the DRI, but after Ellis, Percy, and the fucking cobra were knocked out, he had been, too.

He had woken up in a room one step short of a prison cell. It had a bathroom with a door, a shelf with a serviceable mattress and a pillow, and a table and chair that were bolted to the floor. The bathroom had a security camera, but that was likely a punishment for the grunt assigned to watch him.

Whatever they had drugged him with took a long time to wear off. He had spent most of his time in the cell catching up on sleep.

They had taken his wallet, badge, gun, and pocket knife but not his wristwatch. Several hours after he woke up, he caught himself watching the second hand spin until he was so dizzy he thought about lying down again.

He had missed Mr. Muffins' breakfast, and he was about to miss his dinner. The orange cat was not the forgiving sort. Morrissey shuddered to think about the reception that awaited him. *Maybe I can borrow body armor from the precinct.*

Would he *ever* return home? Liza had uttered the ominous words "organics disposal." Come to think of it, the phrase was an apt description of what Mr. Muffins would do to him.

Morrissey's stomach growled, and he tried the door's handle, which didn't move. He banged on the door until a nervous soldier a decade younger than Charlie cracked it open.

"Can I have something to eat?" Morrissey asked.

The kid peered over his shoulder and frowned, not in anger but in confusion.

"I'll see what I can do." He shut the door.

A hushed conversation sprang up outside. Morrissey caught a few snatches.

"Down to the nutrition lab… Regulations… Care about regulations… Gerbil pellets? No. Check the break room."

Morrissey sighed. The soldiers clearly had not planned on feeding him, which meant they did not keep prisoners. Not for long, anyway.

For the first time, despair curled around his heart. If the DRI killed him, Liza would seriously reconsider her newfound loyalty so his death would not be in vain. She had thought she was doing the right thing. He had seen that "good cop" certainty in her face.

Twenty minutes later, the door opened. Morrissey climbed off his cot and accepted the proffered brown paper bag and red Solo cup of water.

"Thanks." Morrissey took the meal to his table. As the guard shut the door, the other reminded him, "You have to pull the handle, or it won't latch." Morrissey would remember that.

The paper bag contained a turkey sandwich in a Ziploc bag, apple slices, a chocolate chip cookie, and a piece of kitten stationery on which was scribbled in pencil:

Remember,

W goes home alone, and you come home to me.

- C

Morrissey read it three times, trying to decode it, before realizing he was eating someone's lunch. The note must have been from their significant other. The note buoyed his spirits, although it was bittersweet and not meant for him. No one but Mr. Muffins was waiting for *him* at home.

Morrissey polished off the sandwich. The soldiers had mentioned a nutrition lab. What was that about? Maybe part of their training? He bit into the chocolate chip cookie and was distracted from his thoughts.

That night, Morrissey lay on his cot and stared at the ceiling. He was so bored that his skull was about to crumble into dust, so he resorted to constructing a story in his head about the handwritten note from the lunch bag. The love triangle between the soldier, C, and W got more elaborate by the second.

Liza flung the door open and startled him. "What are you reading?"

Morrissey blushed. He was tempted to hide the note, but there was no point. Instead, he waved it at her. "They gave me one of the soldiers' lunches. I guess you guys aren't set up to detain folks."

She looked guilty as she plucked the note from his hand. She snorted when she read it, then muttered, "Wheelwright." She did not return it.

"Are you here to kill me?" Morrissey asked.

Liza frowned. "Do you honestly think I could?"

Morrissey shrugged. "I feel like I don't know you anymore."

"I'm not here to kill you. I would not be the DRI's choice of executioner, anyway." Her voice was hard. "I'm just checking in."

"Mr. Muffins hasn't been fed." The alarm on her face amused him. "Can you feed him for me? And I know this is a lot to ask, but if…if it comes to it, will you take him?"

Mr. Muffins *liked* Liza, which meant he was unlikely to kill her in her sleep. If she accepted, she would have a strong motivation to keep Morrissey alive. He was counting on that.

"Don't be a drama queen." Liza rolled her eyes, but Morrissey knew her body language well enough to understand that she was not as certain as she seemed.

"Are you *actually* here just to check on me, or did you come for a reason?"

Liza hesitated and glanced at the door. Her expression was grim. "I don't know what will happen, but I hope you'll trust me."

When Morrissey opened his mouth to ask her what she meant, she shook her head and glanced at the door again.

She was trying to tell him something, but the guards were listening.

The problem was that Morrissey *didn't* trust Liza now.

"You still keep your spare key in that ridiculous garden gnome?" she asked.

Morrissey nodded. It was unclear whether she was agreeing to feed Mr. Muffins or take custody in the event of his death. She might not have been sure, either.

"Okay." She left.

Charlie waited to hear the click of the latch engaging, but it didn't. After a moment, when no one fixed the problem, a jolt of electricity ran up Morrissey's spine. Liza might not have done so consciously, but she had given him a chance. All he needed now was a distraction. The shift change might work.

He sat on his bed, looking casual and keeping his ears trained on the door. Minutes later, an alarm wailed, and the intercom bleated a pre-recorded message.

"Code Blue. Code Blue. This is not a drill. To your positions. Code Blue, Code Blue…"

The loudspeaker and the sirens made it difficult to hear the agitated conversation between the guards outside his door. He *did*, however, hear their receding footsteps.

Escaping would make it difficult to claim that he was on their side, and he did not know what the alarm meant. A monster could be rampaging through the halls, given how his last few days had gone.

A monster.

Ellis. When he thought about it, the alarm had to do with Ellis. Was she escaping? Had she turned invisible? She had claimed that her powers had diminished, but she had always been quick on her feet. Her injured expression resurfaced in his mind's eye, and Morrissey squared his jaw. Whatever was happening, he would not let her face it alone.

He strode to the door and pushed it. The half-engaged latch scraped in the frame, but the door opened.

Except for the noise, the hall was empty. Morrissey winced at the volume. By now, it would be more of a distraction than an effective warning.

He had no idea where he was or where Ellis was, but he heard screaming to his left. Knowing Ellis' propensity for chaos, he headed toward it.

CHAPTER FOUR

The man in the Corvette's trunk was unhappy. Ellis could not blame him. Having someone hijack your car did not make for a good day.

Ellis had hoped to steal a car in a subtler way, but no opportunities had presented themselves. She had locked the driver in the trunk to delay his ability to report the crime, but it made for a tense trip to the Angeles National Forest. Ellis had learned new and extremely inventive curse words.

Ellis' coughing was bad enough to nauseate her, so Claire drove. Ellis had directed her to one of the homestead's remote entrances, although when the next fit produced blood on the white silk scarf someone had left on the front seat, Ellis questioned the wisdom of her decision.

The entrance was a mile off the road via a poorly maintained game trail. Claire was no longer able to hide her limp, and Ellis was getting worse by the minute. If they went to the main drow entrance instead, they would be able to drive in. However, something kept Ellis from telling her mother to turn around. Claire would have to limp., and Ellis would crawl if she had to.

If Ellis had been able to collect mushrooms from the apartment, she would be healing. Unfortunately, the DRI had made that decision for her.

Ellis pointed at a gravel semicircle off the road. "Stop here."

"There's nothing there," Claire protested.

"We have to walk a little."

"Through the *forest?*"

Talking made her chest hurt, so Ellis just nodded. Claire pulled off, and the undercarriage of the low-slung Corvette scraped on a rock.

Ellis turned to Flower, who was crammed into the space behind the seats, and rasped, "I need your help."

The dog woofed.

Ellis ignored the confusion on her mother's face and offered Flower the keys. "Once we're out of sight, hand these over to the guy, and come find us."

She called through the back seat, "I am going to crack the trunk open. In a few minutes, my dog will drop the keys. If you try to get them before then, you'll be walking back to LA. Do you understand?

"You're crazy, lady!" her captive shouted.

"Probably, but I need to know that you understand."

The man sighed. "Yeah, yeah. I understand."

Ellis popped the trunk, then walked into the woods with Claire.

"He'll call the cops," Claire warned her.

Ellis shrugged. "Even if they believe him, we'll be long

gone when they arrive." As she searched for the start of the game trail, Flower trotted around the car. The keys jingled cheerfully.

"Nice doggie?" the Corvette's owner ventured from inside the trunk. Flower growled.

Ellis found the trail, and they forged ahead. Normally, this was a fifteen-minute cakewalk. Today, it felt like mountaineering. Her breathing sounded like a dying aquarium filter, and Claire's limp made traversing any terrain less even than a sidewalk difficult.

Flower bounded up behind them, then scouted ahead. Ellis smiled. When the faint *creak* of a bowstring being drawn sliced through the rustling leaves and gurgling breaths, Ellis was so relieved that she wanted to cry.

"It's Ellis—" Her throat seized with a coughing fit, and she doubled over.

Nearby plants bent beneath invisible feet. Someone shrouded in shadow magic was approaching. Ellis desperately hoped the drow was her father or Trissa.

Ellis wheezed. "Please. We need help."

Flower barked, ears flattened against her head. Ellis hissed, "Down," and Flower reluctantly slumped to the ground, although her hackles remained erect.

The shadow magic dissolved, and a tall, amethyst-skinned woman stood before her with an arrow nocked. She had dark hair, which was unusual for a drow. Unlike Ellis' raven-wing waves, her hair was a black so light-absorbing that the individual strands were impossible to discern. She wore layered flowing white robes.

Ellis drew another choking breath. "Ilva."

"Where is my son?" the drow demanded. Her dark

eyebrows furrowed, and her purple fingers twitched on the bowstring.

Another coughing fit brought Ellis to her knees. She spat blood on the soil.

Ilva was unmoved. *"Where is Landon?"*

Claire sucked in a breath. "You're—"

Recognition flickered in Ilva's eyes. If looks could kill, Claire would have been flayed on the spot.

"Kill the human." The drow glared at Ellis. "You will return with us to the homestead."

More invisible bowstrings creaked. Ellis threw up her hands and rasped, "You can't! She has information about Landon."

Claire knew the layout of the DRI facility better than Ellis did. Finding Landon would be much easier with her help.

Ilva might have hated Ellis' guts, but she was not stupid. She relaxed the bowstring and returned the arrow to her quiver, then yanked Claire's head up by her chin. "You cannot see the archers, but arrows are still trained on you, human. If you harm us or disobey my orders, they will let fly. Do you understand?"

Ilva's nails left indents in Claire's skin. Drow were stronger than humans, and their longbows could pierce armor.

Claire nodded.

Ellis wheezed. "It's okay, Ilva. She won't hurt anyone. She's my mother."

Claire flinched. Ellis could have sworn that the declaration had embarrassed the woman.

"Ellis needs medical treatment," Claire stated.

Ellis nodded, which made her dizzy. She put a hand on the ground to steady herself, but sunlight reached through the trees and leached what little energy she had left. Flower padded over to support her. "Please. I have to see my father."

Ilva did not respond for a moment. Then, her amethyst face jerked from side-to-side in a curt rejection. "No."

"I have to explain what has happened," Ellis pleaded.

"You *will* explain. To *me*." Ilva fished a rolled leather pouch from her pocket, then unfurled it to reveal a collection of bottles, vials, and herb packets. Ilva selected a bottle, removed the stopper, and handed it to Ellis. It smelled of false lichen and rustcaps.

"Drink it," Ilva commanded. "It will keep the Grasper away."

The Grasper was a drow myth. The long-fingered creature pulled dying drow back to the breast of the Mother Beneath. Ellis was not eager to meet it.

She drained the bottle. Her mouth puckered at the taste, but the liquid was cool in her throat, and the burning in her lungs lessened. Her vision sharpened, and the sun's pressing heat eased. Ellis shivered and climbed to her feet. Flower did not leave her side.

Ilva waved them forward. "Come."

Ilva's archers did not bother to conceal their footsteps, and the forest rustled as they marched. Flower occasionally growled at the archers, but Ellis shushed her.

When Ilva led them past the entrance Ellis had aimed for, she stumbled on a root. Only Flower's quick nudge kept her from falling.

"Where are we going?" Ellis asked. "I thought you were taking us to the—"

Ilva spun and cast a skein of shadow magic around Ellis' face to silence her. She could tell it was shadow magic because she could no longer hear her voice, but she could not feel the magic. She was cut off from its cooling touch.

Ilva's upper lip curled in disgust at the tears that welled in Ellis' eyes. "We will discuss the information you have given this human later. While I draw breath, you will not betray us further. Do you understand?"

Ellis nodded.

Claire came up behind her. "Are you all right?"

Unsure if she was still silenced, Ellis shrugged.

Ellis assumed Ilva was leading them to an emergency bolt hole, but they emerged from the underbrush in front of a cabin. Ellis could hear cars in the distance. They were on the edge of civilization.

Were they breaking into someone's cottage? At first, Ellis was certain that was the case, but then she noticed that the solid stone table in the center of the room was carved in a distinctive drow style—a swirled fungal pattern that had been popular in her father's youth.

She curiously ran her hand over the carved lines. Flower sniffed the underside, then lay down beneath it.

"Come inside," Ilva snapped.

Claire had collapsed on a highbacked chair, pain pinching her face, so the instruction must have been directed at the archers. Footsteps entered the cabin, and Ilva dissolved a magical shroud with a wave.

Ellis gasped. "You *bastard.*"

Errol stood before her. Her brother's ne'er-do-well friend

had betrayed her to the DRI. The attack force he had called in had threatened to kill her and Landon and *had* killed others.

Ellis lunged across the room and wrapped her hand around his throat.

"Release him, or I will remove your hand from your body," Ilva barked.

Ellis gritted her teeth and let go, although she made sure to leave scratches. Under other circumstances, crushing the traitor's windpipe would have been worth it, but she needed her hands to help Landon and Percy.

She rounded on Ilva. "You call *me* a traitor? *He's* the reason Landon was kidnapped. He called the DRI."

"I called them on *you*," Errol argued. "Landon wasn't supposed to be there. I thought they would leave us alone after I turned you in." His defiance was short-lived, and he slumped in agonized regret.

"Errol will face justice," Ilva told her, "but he returned when he did not have to, and he has information we do not."

"Of course he does. He is working for the enemy!"

"And he has seen the error of his ways. His plan to hand you over was…"

"Horrible? Wrong? Evil?"

Ilva scowled. "Poorly thought through. For instance, in the ungentle custody of the enemy, you might have revealed much about the Swallow's Nest."

"Swallow's Nest," Claire quietly repeated. She seemed to be assessing the words for meaning.

Ellis resisted the urge to blurt, "Who's giving up drow secrets now?" Instead, she raised an eyebrow and challenged Ilva. "So, you wouldn't have minded if they killed me as long as they didn't torture me first?"

Ilva flipped a switch, and the overhead lights went on.

Ellis winced and shielded her eyes. "Who pays the electricity bill?"

"You have been through an ordeal," Ilva snapped. "There are beds upstairs. After you have rested, we will eat a meal. After that, we will speak."

"What?" Ellis sputtered. She had expected the woman to beat them senseless. Dinner and a nap was surprisingly soft treatment.

Ilva looked annoyed, with her arms crossed and her eyes narrowed, but she explained, "You are of no use to anyone sun-addled and exhausted." By "anyone," she doubtless meant Landon.

"If you won't take us to my father, will you please send word to him? Or bring him here?" Ellis pleaded. "I need to talk to him."

"No. Connor doesn't need to be involved." Ilva fixed Claire with a stern look, which elicited a flinch.

"You can't keep us here because you're jealous of my mom!" Ellis snapped.

The second the words left her mouth, she regretted them. She expected Ilva to slap or yell at her, but the woman just looked sad.

"You are young and stupid." The words were so sincere that they cut worse than a blow.

Ellis was tempted to protest, to say, "I'm not that young," but her mother wore the same sad look. Ellis huffed and scanned the room, seeking an escape from the argument. She saw no more archers through the windows, only trees.

"Where are the others?" Ellis demanded. "You said there were arrows trained on us."

"There are no others," Ilva replied brusquely.

Ellis' gut twisted uneasily. Surely, Ilva did not expect to save Landon without help. "Only you and Errol, huh? Can't say I think much of your odds."

Ilva raised an eyebrow. "Claire is easily containable when separated from the DRI, and you are not a threat without your shadow magic. You are also both injured."

Ellis wanted to prove her wrong by punching her in the nose, but since she still could not catch her breath, she settled for glaring. "What else are you lying about?"

Ilva sighed. "The only truth I care about is that Landon was kidnapped. Save your energy for saving him."

Ellis wanted to argue more, but her strength had run out. She gazed longingly at Flower, curled into a donut under the table. Her eyes were closed, but her ears were perked.

However infuriating it was, Ilva was right. Ellis was of no use to anyone like this, including herself. She rubbed her eyes and headed for the staircase, wondering if she could make it upstairs. Flower stood and padded after her.

The second floor was a single wood-paneled room. The sparse furnishings were human rather than drow, which was a wise concession. Stone beds on the second floor of an aging cabin would not end well. The only exception was the curtains, which were thick blackout silk.

Ellis relaxed into the shadows, but Claire cursed and

stumbled when she stubbed her toe. Ellis took pity on her mother and eased a curtain open. Light streamed in.

A car flashed past in the distance, accompanied by a whirring noise, but after the car was gone, the noise remained. Ellis opened the curtain more and spotted a black speck above the trees. A bird? It dipped behind an oak and did not reemerge.

Ellis' eyelids drooped of their own accord. If she did not sleep soon, the Grasper might crawl out of the annals of myth and find her.

Two sets of bunk beds lined the walls. Claire had sprawled on a bottom bunk and was snoring. She had not removed her clothing. A cargo pocket near her knee that was held shut by a metal snap bulged. Curious, Ellis crept over.

Claire's eyes shot open, and Ellis guiltily pulled a frayed blue blanket over her mother's shoulders. Claire murmured something and closed her eyes again.

When the black shapes slipped through the forest to besiege the cabin, Ellis was asleep.

CHAPTER FIVE

The DRI facility was an oppressive taupe maze. Morrissey kept hoping to stumble upon a brightly lit mall-style map with helpful labels like Nutrition Lab and Illegally Detained Prisoners, but he was disappointed by the locked doors and endless hallways.

Footsteps approached behind him. Morrissey tried the next doorknob, but it was locked like all the others. It was no use. They would catch him.

Before Morrissey joined the homicide division, he had solved a string of burglaries. The burglar's method had been simple. He went to fancy parties, acted as though he had been invited, then melted into the throng and took whatever struck his fancy. Once, he cut a Monet out of its frame and walked out with the rolled-up painting under his arm. Confidence could be an extremely effective disguise.

Morrissey forced himself to relax his shoulders, then accelerated to a brisk walk appropriate for the blaring sirens. It was hard to make out the nearing conversation.

"MEC escaped."

"Boss thinks it's in the vents."

Morrissey caught his breath at the word "escape." The sirens had started *before* he had left his cell, not after, and judging from the size of the grates, he doubted anyone would think him capable of climbing into them. Ellis could have. Was Ellis the "it" in the vent, or were they talking about the cobra?

Morrissey kept his gait steady as the soldiers caught up. There were four, and all wore full-face helmets.

The man in the lead rumbled, "You're not in kit, man. Code Blue means full silks."

"Full silks" sounded like the dress code for a brothel, not an army, but Morrissey nodded and replied, "Yes, sir."

The soldier behind the leader stepped forward. "I don't recognize you." Morrissey was surprised to realize it was a woman.

He tried to look embarrassed as he grasped for an explanation. He knew so little about this place. "It's my second day. I'm trying to find the nutrition lab. Bad luck, huh?"

He put on a goofy, self-deprecating smile and prayed. It was a wild swing. If the woman stepped any closer, she would hear his heart pounding against his ribcage.

"Aw, you'll be okay," she replied soothingly. "Remember your door protocol."

"You said you were going to the nutrition lab?" The leader was harsher than the woman. He was obviously less interested in nurturing a positive work environment.

Morrissey's stomach flipped. He had no idea if the

claim was credible. "Special project. Am I even going the right way? I am *totally* turned around."

"Take two rights, and you'll see it. Kit up before the doc sees you."

Morrissey nodded. Whoever "the doc" was, Morrissey hoped he would not meet the person. The man led his crew away and threw an irritated glance over his shoulder. Irritated was good. Morrissey was happy to play the part of an incompetent greenhorn.

When the knot of soldiers disappeared around the next corner, Morrissey let out his breath in a *whoosh*. He had only talked his way out because the soldiers had been distracted by the alert. He would not be able to bluff a second time.

He had to find an exit. He took the two rights as had been suggested, which led him to a door labeled Nutrition, but he did not enter. He continued searching for a staircase or an elevator but found nothing.

Footsteps thundered down the corridor. Had someone finally noticed he was missing?

The nutrition lab was as good a place to hide as any, so he retraced his steps at a jog. He opened the door, praying his luck would hold, and sagged with relief when it was empty. He locked the door behind him. It would not keep trouble out forever, but it might buy him a few precious minutes.

The room looked like an industrial kitchen, with stainless steel countertops and wooden butcher block counters. He assumed the heavy steel door on one wall opened into a walk-in freezer. Metal racks on another wall held plastic tubs of small brown pellets with lists of macronutrients taped to the outside. Morrissey read one.

Subject ADC—increased protein content. Vitamin D withheld.

He popped the lid open and sniffed. A faint cat food odor wafted out. That explained why the soldiers had given him one of their lunches. This place was not set up to feed people.

The blare of the siren was quieter in here, but it was still loud enough to cover the click of claws on the smooth tile. When a sharp pain pierced his ankle, he stifled a yelp. He expected to see the king cobra when he looked down, but a small ball of orange and white fur hissed at him.

It was a guinea pig—an *angry* one. Morrissey withdrew his foot before the creature could sink its long teeth into his ankle again. "Hey, knock it off!"

The guinea pig chittered and dove for Morrissey's other ankle. He did not want to kick it, so he hopped onto the counter. The guinea pig screeched and vainly attempted to follow.

Morrisey inspected his ankle. The guinea pig had drawn blood. "What the hell?" he whispered.

A ridiculous thought struck him. What if *this* was what the soldiers were looking for? It was small enough to enter a vent. It did not *appear* to pose a significant threat, but Morrissey had no idea what kind of research went on here. They could be studying the effects of infectious diseases on guinea pigs.

A tub of pellets was within reach. Morrissey emptied its contents onto the counter, then flipped it and dropped it over the bouncing guinea pig.

Morrissey put his foot on the tub to keep the rodent from shoving it across the floor, then stretched to retrieve a second tub of kibbles. He withdrew his foot and hastily placed the second tub on top of the first. That would hold…for now.

The ball of fur repeatedly threw itself against the walls of its prison.

Can guinea pigs catch rabies? Morrissey wished he had Internet access.

He washed his ankle in the sink, then watched the puncture wounds for a full two minutes, waiting for them to break out in boils or angry red lines to announce the delivery of a biohazard into his bloodstream. Maybe he would develop an intense craving for brains.

Instead, the blood clotted, and the pain lessened. Morrissey glowered at the guinea pig, which was still squealing. "You should meet my cat. You'd get along great."

He searched the lab for anything to improve his chance of survival, pocketing a paring knife. He left a cleaver within reach on the counter.

Morrissey leafed through a notebook he found on the counter with great interest. The pages contained no admissions of transmittable diseases harbored by the local wildlife, only formulas for the food assigned to alphanumerically labeled subjects. He wondered which one the guinea pig was.

Finally, he turned to the walk-in freezer. Something hummed as he unlatched and unsealed the door. To his surprise, the hum turned into a furious buzz when he pulled the door open.

The smell hit him next, and Morrissey's jaw dropped as

automatic fluorescent lights clicked on overhead. This was not a walk-in freezer; it was an animal lab. Perhaps "containment area" was a better choice of words.

The long, narrow space's walls were covered with cages from floor to ceiling. The larger ones had metal bars, and the smaller ones were fronted with mesh. A bright blue bird strutted and squawked in the nearest cage. Its claws reminded Morrissey of the paring knife in his pocket.

It stared at Morrissey before turning its attention to an enclosure full of rats on the other side of the room. The rats stared back, shrieking and scrabbling at the mesh.

Were the thick metal doors there to keep people out or to keep the animals in? Morrissey shivered and walked on.

Three-quarters of the way down the hall, he spied a guinea pig-sized hole in a mesh-fronted cage. When he bent to inspect it, something moved in the shadowy cage beside it. A spider the size of a small dog clicked across the floor and into the light.

Morrissey's heart jumped. He had seen similar spiders in the hall with Ellis and Percy, but he had been too panicked to examine them. Now, he could take a closer look.

The spider was beautiful. Its segmented eyes glistened with rainbows, and its ebony torso gleamed like glass. Its legs were elegant, and its talons glittered dangerously.

Unbidden, Morrissey's hand moved toward the latch, but a growl broke his concentration. He fell back as the spider leaped at the metal bars with its fangs bared. The bars of another cage hit his back, and something clawed through his blazer and drew blood.

He rolled away and lay on the white tile. The black

jaguar that had wounded him roared and swiped at the bars again. Its cage was too small for it, and its cries chilled Morrissey more than the climate control. *What the hell is this place?*

This did not seem like a normal lab. If they were testing products on animals, he would have expected a homogeneous population. He was not a scientific genius, but he knew enough from forensics coursework to understand the concept of a sample size. Whatever experiments these animals were undergoing were unlikely to show up in legitimate journals.

His back itched more than it hurt. The jaguar had only scratched him. He clambered to his feet and continued toward the exit, which was identical to the entrance. He put his hand on the latch but hesitated when he heard the first door opening.

Panic seized him. He hauled on the latch, hoping to slip through before he could be caught, but it was locked.

He cursed under his breath and turned to face his fate. There was no cover in this narrow space. Shooting him would be easier than shooting fish in a barrel.

Liza stepped into the lab. She was alone, and she held her gun loosely at her side. She said Morrissey's name with a relieved sigh.

Morrissey glared at her. "Are you going to shoot me?"

"I hope not." Liza strode down the hall. "I was coming to visit you. How did you escape? I didn't see any... bodies."

"The door to that cell doesn't latch."

She scowled. "It's not a cell. It's for employees working long shifts or visitors."

"Anything's a cell if you put guards outside and lock the doors."

Liza shook her head. "You wouldn't say that if you knew what the cells in this place looked like. I managed to keep you out of those, so don't fuck me over."

He crossed his arms. "What's going on with the alarm? Did an animal escape?"

An inscrutable look passed over Liza's face before she sighed. "The alarm is for your pet vigilante."

"Where is she?"

"Rein in your steed, Mr. Knight in Shining Armor," Liza snarled. She drew a deep breath and attempted a reasonable tone. "You can't help her if you're dead, and I'm your best shot at staying alive."

Morrissey grimaced. "This place is evil, Liza. Can't you feel it? Something is wrong with these animals."

She scanned the rows of cages, and to his surprise, she nodded. "Believe me, I know. I don't like the DRI any more than you do, but they have their claws in me."

Morrissey could relate. The lines of fire the jaguar had raked in his back still burned. "I thought you had more backbone."

"I've been getting the lay of the land," Liza retorted. She was less friendly, but Morrissey was too angry to let up.

"The DRI killed innocent people." Ellis had told him about the attack on the compound in Topanga Canyon. Several men and women had been killed.

"I did what I could to help her," Liza protested. "The people who died..."

"The people the DRI *killed*," Morrissey corrected.

She shrugged helplessly. "They told us that they'd been

taken over by the enemy. That the MECs had hypnotized them, and they weren't really *people* anymore."

"What does MEC stand for?"

"Metaphysically enhanced combatant," Liza admitted after a pause. "Like your vigilante friend, except…"

"What?"

"She can speak."

Morrissey blinked. "Of course she can fucking speak. She's a human being."

"The purple ones can't."

Morrissey thought back to the purple woman who had blown the top off his car at the bluegrass concert. "Yes, they can."

Liza's face paled. "What are you talking about? Did you encounter another MEC?"

"More than one. They were kind of rude to me."

Liza's breath was speeding up. "The director told us they're not human. They *look* human, but the likeness is superficial. He told us the MECs are like rabid dogs."

Morrissey thought about the pellets in the nutrition lab. Was that what they'd fed Ellis? Fury surged inside him, and he grabbed Liza's collar. "You fell for their bullshit. Where are you holding them?"

She opened her mouth to respond but was interrupted by a click behind them. The door that had been locked swung open.

"Director," Liza murmured. Fear blossomed in her eyes.

Morrissey let go of Liza's collar and turned. The man who had entered was short, and he wore a green lab coat patterned in paisley with a purple bow tie and alligator boots. Despite his stature and ridiculous outfit, he oozed authority. His dark eyes seemed to swallow the available light. More alarmingly, the cacophony died when he stepped in since the animals shrank back into the recesses of their cages in unison.

Morrissey's guts knotted. The last time a man had made him feel this way, he had been interviewing the LA River Killer, who had murdered six people over a decade.

The thought made him shiver, but he was unsure of why his subconscious had drawn the comparison. When Morrissey looked at the man's face, déjà vu enveloped him. The structure of his face was familiar.

The director did not pick up on Morrissey's unease, or if he did, he did not mention it. His posture was relaxed. "You're new."

"Charlie Morrissey. LAPD. Your people have my badge somewhere."

The man's eyebrows twitched. "I see you've effected a jailbreak. I thought I asked the boys to keep an eye on you."

Liza spoke carefully. "Charlie, this is Dr. Malcolm Millwright, the director of the DRI. Morrissey didn't break out, sir. I asked him for help. Sebastian told me one of your animals had escaped while they were taking its stats, and they didn't have time to round it up. Morrissey and I worked together for a long time at the police department. He's trustworthy. Everyone else was busy responding to the code blue, so… I conscripted him as my backup."

"You thought a guinea pig was a two-man job?" Nothing in his voice suggested that he was angry, but his gaze was ice-cold.

"Don't count the guinea pig out. Next time, you might want to call the National Guard," Morrissey muttered.

Liza shot Morrissey a sharp look. "I will admit I didn't realize Seb was talking about a guinea pig. The animal subjects are notoriously vicious. From the way he described the behavior, I thought it was something bigger."

Morrissey held back a shudder at the prospect of a dog being kept in this cold, lonely basement. Even a cat man like him recognized that injustice.

"The guinea pig did bite me," Morrissey offered.

The director did not look alarmed. Morrissey assumed that if he had been exposed to a novel pathogen, his statement would have elicited a response. However, given the chill Morrissey felt when he met the man's gaze, the director might regard the bleeding eyeballs of an Ebola patient with the same impersonal expression as a runny nose.

"Then I suppose thanks are in order for your assistance in rounding up such a vicious and terrifying beast." Millwright's tone was light as a feather. "Please accept my condolences for your battle wounds. Shall I put you up for a Purple Heart?"

The sarcasm was so thick that Morrissey did not bother to respond.

"Sir, the MEC?" Liza murmured.

Millwright speared her with a glare. In a low, icy voice, he told her, "Despite your personal feelings about Mr. Morrissey, he does not have security clearance. I will thank you not to discuss issues of importance with him."

Liza straightened. Her professionalism clearly warred with her sense of camaraderie, but she barked, "Yes, sir."

Playing by the rules had gotten her far in the LAPD, but

it would not save her from this quagmire. Morrissey wondered if she knew that.

Millwright's features softened as she snapped to attention, but the thaw did not extend to his eyes. Morrissey's skin prickled as the man smiled. "Come into my office. Perhaps we can resolve Detective Morrissey's situation."

Millwright missed nothing. When Charlie exhaled in relief, Millwright's nostrils flared in disgust. His smile remained frozen, however, and he led them through the other door. As it turned out, it opened into his office.

When Liza shut the thick metal door behind them, the chorus of animal screams resumed.

CHAPTER SIX

Ellis was roughly shaken awake. When Errol's face swam into view, she instinctively rolled out of the bed. She hit the floor shoulder-first and grasped for the shadows under the bed. As usual, they eluded her.

"The cabin's under attack," Errol snapped.

The words were slow to penetrate Ellis' sleepy haze. She could not remember her dreams, but her mouth tasted like acid, so she guessed they had been nightmares.

Errol hauled her to her feet. Ellis caught sight of Claire's rumpled, empty bed and gasped.

"She's downstairs," Errol sharply replied.

Ellis hurried to the window and flicked open the curtain, and the glass shattered inward as a gunshot rang out.

She yanked the blackout silk curtain in front of her to shield herself and yelled, "*Get down!*" but Errol was already on the floor. At first, she feared he had been shot, but he then rolled over to face her.

He stared at the window. "They have snipers."

Thank you, Captain Obvious. "You betrayed us," she hissed. "*Again.*"

Errol shook his head. "Your mother must have called them."

"What the hell are you talking about?"

He gave her a pitying look. "Come on, Ellis. You can't possibly be this stupid. She's playing you."

Footsteps came up the stairs, and Errol snapped his mouth shut as Claire appeared.

Her gaze first went to the shards of glass on the floor, then Ellis. Pain creased her face. "Ellis! Thank goodness you're all right."

Errol's accusation was unthinkable. Claire appeared to be genuinely worried by the prospect of snipers. Then again, Ellis recalled Claire touching her ear and saying something while they were outside the apartment complex. Had she been wearing an earpiece, or had she been speaking to an onlooker, and the gesture was a coincidence?

If she wanted to betray me, she wouldn't have rescued me.

Ellis army-crawled to the stairs, and the three snuck down to the lower level, which was empty of everything but shadows. Ellis frowned and briefly wondered where Ilva had gone until she saw the latch on a forest-facing window slide open.

Of course, idiot. She disappeared the second she heard trouble.

Ellis could not sense Ilva's shadow magic. That embarrassed her. Ilva already thought of her as the bastard child who had damaged her relationship with Connor. She did not need more reason to think poorly of Ellis.

The window slid up, and another shot rang out. The bullet hole appeared on the far wall, and Ellis slumped in relief. It had not hit Ilva.

Gunfire sprayed through the open window. Ellis ran to the stone table, tipped it onto its side, and rolled it in front of the doorway. It would double as a barrier against invaders and a shield against bullets.

Invisible footsteps approached, and a cool hand touched her arm. Ilva's voice emanated from the air beside Ellis. "We must tunnel. You will help me."

Ellis understood. The DRI was covering the doors and windows, so they would have to escape through the ground. The tunneling spell was not complex, but it required the participation of three or more drow. Even if they could trust Errol, which was a *big* if, he was not much of a mage.

Too bad I'm not either right now.

Ilva was clearly frightened. Ellis guessed the fear was more for Landon than herself. She was glad she could not see the older woman's face as she guiltily whispered, "I'm sorry, but I can't help."

Ilva growled in frustration. "You would rather betray your brother and hand us over to the enemy?"

"No," Ellis protested. "I *can't* help. The soldiers out there have access to lightsilk that's stronger than ours. It burns, and it drained my powers."

"What?" Claire hissed. She crawled toward the table at high speed, and before Ellis could stop her, she ran into Ilva's invisible form. Disgust flashed across her mother's face. She wiped the expression away, but Ellis had seen it.

Was her mother *that* repulsed by shadow magic? The next volley of bullets interrupted her pondering.

"You told no one about this injury?" Ilva demanded. "How could you fail to warn the drow of this threat?"

"I was dealing with it," Ellis defensively replied. "Landon knew. He was helping me."

Ellis' ear was assaulted by an angry huff. "I *see*."

Claire anxiously glanced past Ellis at the door. "There are too many of them. You have to surrender. You're valuable to their research." Her voice was choked with shame.

"That is precisely why we cannot allow ourselves to be taken." Ilva's tone was icily certain. "Whatever the cost, they must not take us alive. There is no shame in joining the Mother Beneath, but those people are evil. Our bodies might unwittingly betray our people."

Errol crawled into the shelter of the table. "Let me distract them," he whispered. "I'll go through the door and let them see me, then draw them away. You can sneak through behind me under Ilva's shroud. While they're busy with me, you can make it into the woods."

Ellis stared at him. The proposition was suicidal. Errol was among her brother's oldest friends. He was a delinquent, prone to idiotic crimes, but he had also been brave enough to leave the homestead and make a life in the outside world.

Landon might never have left the homestead without Errol's influence. Her brother would not have been kidnapped if he had not left home, but Ellis' and Landon's exposure to the human world had helped them understand one another. It had brought them closer together, transforming their relationship from annoyance to allies.

Ellis grabbed Errol's arm. "There has to be another way."

He shook his head sadly. His haunted expression spoke of a man leaning over the abyss.

"He sacrifices himself, or we all die," Ilva stated. Then, softening from diamond to sandstone, she added, "I accept your proposal, Errol. You will redeem yourself before you join the Mother Beneath."

"No," Claire muttered, then repeated it more loudly. "No. Give me a piece of your robe."

"Why?"

"You're the only one who's wearing white."

Silence.

"If this doesn't work, I won't argue, and we'll try Errol's way," Claire pleaded, "but we have to escape this trap. We don't *have* to die to do so."

Ellis interpreted Ilva's silence as a lack of enthusiasm about allowing Claire to take the reins, but a moment later, fabric tore and a pale purple hand emerged from thin air, holding a dinner plate-sized white rag.

Claire crawled over to a broom resting against the wall. She knotted the fabric onto the handle, then returned to the stone table, cautiously unlatched the door, and shoved the flag through the gap.

A hail of bullets struck the door. Ellis cowered behind the table with her hands over her ears, but Claire kept waving the broom handle. The flag had to be in tatters.

Finally, the gunfire ebbed. Ellis closed her eyes and breathed a sigh of relief. When she opened them again, Claire stood in the open doorway with her hands above her head. Ellis was frozen in place. By the time Ellis had the wherewithal to reach for her mother, Claire had walked out. Ellis made to scramble after her, but Ilva pulled her back.

Shouts of recognition came from farther off, and heavy footsteps crunched through the undergrowth. The man they belonged to seemed confused when he spoke. "Doc? What are you doing here?"

Doc?

"There's been a misunderstanding," Claire told him, then snapped, "What are you doing?"

"Door protocol," the soldier replied. He went past Claire and through the door, and a loud *bang* came on the heels of his pronouncement. Ellis recognized the noise from the night the DRI had killed Morrissey's captain. The soldier had fired a lightsilk confetti gun.

Scraps of burning silk floated through the air. Most fell short of the table, but a few stray threads floated above Ilva's head with deadly languor. Ellis snatched them and pressed her lips together against the pain as the lightsilk burned her skin.

"I saw something!" he barked.

Ellis grimaced and prayed the risk would be worth it. Ilva's invisibility shroud could be their ticket out.

Claire's response dripped irritation. "That's the new research assistant I personally recruited from MIT. If you scare the shit out of her, I will lose her to Silicon Valley."

"But—"

"No *buts.* Stand *down.*"

That was an order, not a request. For someone who had not worked at the DRI in two decades, Claire was very confident that she would be obeyed. Ellis' suspicions were multiplying.

Boots shuffled, then the soldier clicked his radio, and static buzzed. "Stand down. There's been a misunderstanding." The radio clicked off. "Sorry, Doc. We thought—"

"Keep your thoughts to yourself," Claire interrupted him. "If you'll excuse me, I expect I need to find a terrified grad student a new pair of pants."

"Yes, Doc." The soldier walked out, murmuring orders into his radio.

"We must *go*," Ilva whispered. The air blurred. Ellis could not feel it but knew that Ilva had extended her shroud.

They snuck out of the cabin in an invisible knot. The fresh air was a welcome relief from the clinging stench of fear. When Ilva strode toward the tree line to the east, away from Claire, Ellis gripped her arm.

"Wait," she begged. "We can't leave my mother."

"We certainly can."

Ilva was right, but Ellis remained pinned to the spot. "Fine, then. I *won't* leave my mother. She saved our lives."

"Ask yourself *why* she would do that."

"Because she's my mother."

"You know nothing about her."

Anger made her skin prickle, although Ellis was unsure if she was angry because Ilva was right or because she was wrong. She gritted her teeth. "I know what she did for us. I'm going back for her."

"They will probably shoot you." Ilva sounded unbothered.

Claire had gone back into the cabin and was searching

for something, possibly Ellis. Five soldiers milled around the cabin, armed with guns and lightsilk nets. The sun was dipping below the tree line. Its burnt-orange glow would soon fade.

"We wait until it's dark, then bring her out through there." Ellis pointed at the shattered window, then crouched in the field and pinned Errol with a glare. "After everything you said, you went back to the homestead."

He ducked his head. "I thought it was my duty to help Landon. I thought I was doing what was best for all of us."

"You were never concerned about *all* of us," Ellis retorted.

He crossed his legs and did not respond.

Waiting in the open in an invisible cluster was tense but boring. Ellis was relieved when the last of the daylight faded. The remaining soldiers left.

They shuffled to the window inside Ilva's envelope of shadow magic.

"Are you muffling our voices?" Ellis murmured to Ilva.

"You cannot tell?" Ilva sounded surprised and curious, not judgmental, but Ellis' cheeks still burned.

Tears welled in her eyes, and she shook her head. "I couldn't use shadow magic when I was first burned by the lightsilk. Now I can't even feel it."

Ilva grasped her hand and examined the red marks left by the strands of silk. Cool magic washed over Ellis' skin, and the red marks faded.

"Thanks," Ellis whispered.

Ilva nodded. "To answer your question, yes, our voices are muffled."

Ellis drew a deep breath and let it out slowly. "Okay. I'll get my mom. Can you let me talk to her?"

A light flicked on in the cabin. Even under the shroud, it was painfully bright. Claire stood at the window and squinted through Ellis, Errol, and Ilva.

"Mom?" Ellis tentatively asked.

Claire froze. Ellis thought the invisible voice had alarmed her, but then she realized it was the first time Ellis had called her "Mom." Ellis chastised herself, but she could not retract it.

"Climb out and join us," Ellis whispered.

Claire eyed the pane's jagged edge. Ilva sighed, raised a finger, and smoothed the shards to nubs as harmless as sea glass. Fear flashed across Claire's face, but she climbed over. As she did, Ilva extended the shroud to include her, and upon seeing the group, she gasped.

"I thought you left."

"I am surprised you stayed," Ilva replied.

Claire hesitated halfway over the sill and looked at the trees. "I thought leaving would raise suspicion. Someone might still be watching."

"If they are, they can't see you anymore." Ellis grabbed her mother's arm and helped her through the window.

"You're strong," Claire exclaimed, not in admiration but in fear.

Ellis did not reply. The confirmation that her mother was afraid of her sent a cold bolt down her spine.

"We should move," Ilva brusquely informed them.

She led them back the way they had come. It was a tedious trek since Ilva refused to divulge their destination. At last, they stopped in a small clearing.

"Walk the perimeter," Ilva ordered Ellis. "Flush out any humans who are concealing themselves."

Ilva was the Homestead's best weaponsmith. Her apprentices consumed her words as though they were oxygen, and she was not accustomed to being disobeyed. It was vaguely validating that Ilva trusted her to check the perimeter rather than Errol. Granted, nobody trusted Errol.

Claire slumped to the ground and massaged her knee. Ellis considered whether Ilva would harm her while Ellis was gone, then realized the drow woman could have done so at any time.

Before Ellis could leave, Ilva handed her a small silk pouch. Ellis opened it and grinned at the dense, crumbling rectangle inside. It was a tunnel bar.

Drow miners drilled for days at a time. To sustain themselves, they brought tunnel bars. Tunnel bars were cut from dried and pressed blocks of nourishing, stimulating mushrooms.

The first bite flooded Ellis with homesickness and energy. She was wired and emotionally exhausted, a great combination.

She remembered feeling this sad in childhood. At the time, she had believed that having a mother would solve all her problems. Now, she had one, but she felt no different.

For the umpteenth time, she missed her father. If she abandoned her perimeter walk, she could reach the homestead in less than a day.

A twig snapped beneath her foot, and something screamed in the forest.

Ellis froze. The scream had come from the clearing. Maybe she had been too quick to trust Ilva.

She sprinted back. Leaping over logs and launching herself off boulders until her thighs burned, she thanked the Mother Beneath for the tunnel bar.

Ellis' stomach turned when she arrived. Starlight illuminated the scene. Errol had Claire pinned, and Ilva was roughly searching her clothes. It was silent. Ilva must have muffled the noise with shadow magic.

Ellis hurdled a bush and screamed, "*Stop!*"

The drow woman spun, then rolled off Claire. In response to Ellis' raised fists, Ilva drew a long, thin blade from her boot and curled the fingers of her other hand into a claw. Ellis saw nothing but presumed the other woman held a ball of shadow magic.

Claire looked rattled but unharmed. Ilva nodded at Errol, who released her. Claire's lips moved, but the muffling magic was still in effect.

"*What the hell?*" Ellis demanded of Ilva.

Ilva sighed. "You *must* see that your misplaced feelings have clouded your judgment."

Her cool, reasonable tone fanned Ellis' fury. "You were hurting her," Ellis accused.

"I was not."

Ellis looked at Claire. The lines on her face were deeper, and the dark circles under her eyes were visible in the starlight. She did not appear injured, but she *did* seem ashamed.

"We were searching her," Errol volunteered.

"A fruitful search." Ilva removed a small black object

from her pocket. "Errol tells me this device reveals our location to distant individuals."

Ellis snatched it. For all of its earth-shattering importance, it was made of cheap black plastic. A light flashed red inside a seam in the tiny box. She scowled. "How do *you* know? You can barely use a cell phone!"

Errol miserably hung his head. "I've used them. I'm shit at shadow magic, but I can plant something on someone who doesn't know any better."

"Enough." Ilva waved her hand, and the tracker dissolved into the night air.

Ellis stared at Claire, desperate to find denial in her face. Maybe the tracker had been in the stolen uniform. "Mom, tell them they're wrong!"

Claire again winced at the word "Mom." The reaction burned worse than lightsilk. "I don't know how it got there." She did not sound convincing.

Ellis' heart sank. It *was* a tracker.

"We can handle culpability later," Ilva cut in. "Right now, what is most important is that more soldiers will come to this place."

"I didn't see anyone on my perimeter walk," Ellis reported.

Ilva shrugged. "Your senses are deadened. I sent you out as a diversion."

Ellis had fallen for it. She glared. She had to stay angry. If she did not, she would start wondering why her mother had a tracker in her pocket and had been able to dismiss the DRI soldiers with a word.

Ellis loomed over her mother. "Those soldiers knew you. Why?"

"When they called me in about your blood sample, I met a few people…"

"Your *blood* sample?" Ilva repeated in alarm.

Ellis impatiently waved a hand. "I was a ghost. It is a long story."

Claire was desperate. "I had to make friends again so I could find you. The DRI has expanded since I was there."

Ilva scoffed. Her eyes reminded Ellis of shattered glass. "Ellis' vision might be clouded, but mine is as clear as a cave pool. If you were unfamiliar to these men, they would not have left. It takes a great deal of authority to turn back people with powerful weapons."

Something hummed in the distance. Ellis shushed the others and focused. It was the same noise she had heard at the cabin. "I hear a drone."

Muttering curses that would burn the ears of the Mother Beneath, Ilva stretched out her hands, and the pale starlight rippled into silvery lines. Another shadow magic shroud.

Minutes passed in silence until the dark shape of a drone crossed the tree line and hovered above the clearing. Ilva nocked an arrow as Ellis peered at the mesh bag dangling beneath the drone. It caught the moonlight and glittered.

She grabbed Errol's and Ilva's arms. *"Lightsilk!"*

They reached the tree line a heartbeat before the bag exploded. Ilva had abandoned the shadow shroud, and the lightsilk strands floated over Claire like tinsel. Claire brushed the threads away and stared at the drone's camera.

Ilva drew, then loosed an arrow. It struck true, and the drone crashed to the ground.

"We have to go," Ellis urged.

"We should destroy the drone first," Errol protested.

Ellis shook her head. "Look."

The drone was sparking on the ground. Now that it was still, the sheen on the propellers was unmistakable. The machine was covered in lightsilk, stretched over wire frames. Another tracker flashed red on the drone's under-carriage.

Flower, who had followed Ellis into the trees, growled at the downed drone. That gave Ellis an idea. She raised her hands over her head and clapped three times.

CHAPTER SEVEN

The zoological body count in Millwright's office rivaled the most successful hunting lodge. Glassy eyes watched from every surface and corner, from cervid heads on the walls to stuffed game birds to trout mounted on plaques. The worst was a thick black snake curled around a large branch in the corner behind the desk.

Only the back wall was devoid of taxidermy. It showcased an oil painting depicting a pitched battle between tigers and Roman gladiators. The blood on the sand was so well-rendered that the paint looked wet.

The bloody décor should not have been enough to raise goosebumps on the back of Charlie's neck and turn his stomach. Morrissey did not hunt, but many of his friends did. He had never felt this way about his buddies' hobby.

Morrissey realized the source of his discomfort as Millwright droned. The trophy mounts' cold, dead eyes were identical to those of the living animals in the lab. The jaguar might have had better mobility, but it was dead inside.

"So, Detective Morrissey. What do you think?"

The beady eyes' unblinking void persisted. Charlie could not tear his gaze away.

Liza's fingers brushed his arm, and the hint of warmth broke his trance.

"What?" he blurted.

Liza glared at him. Morrissey turned back to Millwright. Again, the man's face gave him déjà vu. Had the DRI collaborated with the LAPD in the past? They occasionally worked with the FBI, so it was not inconceivable for him to have encountered the DRI in a back-channel capacity.

The connection continued to elude him. His gaze was drawn back to the stuffed snake. Something was off about it.

The snake blinked.

Morrissey yelped and shied away. His chair tilted dangerously, and Liza brought him back to the floor with a *thud,* although her expression curdled when she realized what he had been staring at. She was less blatant about inching away.

It was not a trophy mount. It was Percy's fucking cobra.

Millwright smiled. It made his face look like an over-ripe fruit split in two. He tented his fingers on the desk and favored the snake with an indulgent look. "I forgot to thank you, Detective, for bringing me this lavish gift."

"No problem." Charlie scooted his chair back another foot.

The rotten-fruit smile grew. "Come now, Detective. A snake won't attack for no reason, and were I to give it a reason, you wouldn't be far enough away."

Millwright seemed relaxed despite being within easy striking distance. Was he threatening Charlie or warning him? Before Morrissey could puzzle it out, Millwright repeated his earlier question. "What do you think?"

"About what?"

Liza's hand twitched in a manner Charlie associated with wanting to stab someone.

Millwright sighed. "About the job. What do you think about the *job?*"

Liza nudged his leg. "It'll be like the old days. Remember the raid on Dirty RJ's garage?"

Unease swirled within her cheerful tone. Charlie struggled to remember a raid on something called "Dirty RJ's Garage." A black-market chop shop?

With a start, he realized she was referring to Ron Jackson. Why would she veil the reference? Did Liza know or suspect that Jackson had been involved with the DRI?

Her expression was serious. This must have been the conversation she had wanted to have in the lab. She wanted to finish it without revealing her hand.

What are you telling me, Liza?

"Here, we could clean up those sorts of things together." Her gaze was the sharpest dagger, and she had emphasized the words "clean up."

Morrissey kept his face pleasant as he parsed the implication. She was telling him the DRI was corrupt, and she wanted him to take it down with her.

He considered his options. If he turned Millwright down, there was a significant chance that he would not make it out of this complex alive.

"And if I say no?" Morrissey lightly inquired. "I'm kind of partial to Homicide."

"So am I," Millwright replied. He held Charlie's gaze for a moment, laughing when Morrissey awkwardly cleared his throat. "Please, Charlie. Surely you're not afraid I'd have you killed? Cover-ups are too much work.

"If you say no, you will sign NDAs to the effect that disclosing anything you've learned about the DRI, including its existence, will be considered treason against the United States government. As you no doubt know, that is a capital offense. Back you go to your job in Homicide and your delightful orange cat. It relies on you for protection."

Any reasonable person would have interpreted it as a threat, but Morrissey suspected Millwright was complimenting Mr. Muffins. That made him even *more* reluctant.

Millwright could also be lying. "Organics disposal" came to mind.

Then again, he would never learn what "organics disposal" was if he did not stick around, and Liza was a straight shooter. She evidently thought she could do some good here.

Morrissey imagined returning to the LAPD and walking around the city, knowing the DRI was carrying out unspeakable experiments. Knowing this place existed, and he had done nothing about it.

Morrissey forced an ironic grin. "What kind of vacation time am I looking at?"

Color returned to Liza's cheeks, and Millwright chuckled. "You'll find it competitive."

Now that he was reasonably certain he was not facing

imminent death, Morrissey's mind raced with possibilities. His favorite option was simple. He had not passed a single emergency exit sign. The LA fire marshal would have a field day with this place.

Millwright tapped a finger on his desk, and the snake twisted around its post. "Normally, I would bring you in for a full orientation, but you don't need to push through the barrier of disbelief about the little purple men living under Los Angeles."

Morrissey snorted. "They're not *that* little."

"Yes, well, neither are they men," Millwright dryly added. "Agent L, take him to procurement. Kit him out for a guard shift, but don't issue him a service weapon yet."

Morrissey's dream of returning with a triumphant brigade of firemen disappeared quicker than Ellis in a snit. Millwright would keep him down here and test his loyalty. If he did not pass with flying colors, it would be easy to orchestrate an accident.

He was not claustrophobic, but he abruptly felt as though the entirety of Los Angeles was bearing down on him. Would he ever see the sun again?

Showing fear would not help. The air seemed to thicken to an unbreathable miasma and his world spun as he allowed Liza to pull him from the room.

CHAPTER EIGHT

When the door closed behind the two LAPD transplants, Director Malcolm Millwright sat quietly. Morrissey had been lying, but to whom?

If Morrissey was lying to Millwright, he would soon give himself away. Malcolm had a range of solutions for that. If Morrissey was lying to himself, he would be unpredictable.

DRI recruitment was a treacherous tightrope. "Good cops" rarely had the stomach for it. Millwright foresaw half a dozen ways in which Liza might attempt to befoul his plans.

On the other hand, "bad cops" cheated, stole, and pissed off their coworkers. Ron Jackson had been a low-level informant, but he had sown incredible chaos. While the man had not been stupid, he had selected his allies based on blind personal loyalty rather than competence. Therefore, he had been surrounded by idiots.

One of Jackson's cronies had taken photos of two MECs and attempted to sell them to the *National Enquirer*.

Fortunately, the editor had dismissed them as fakes, but the magazine's staff still occasionally used the photos in memes, such as a picture of a purple man captioned "Holding my breath for the return of print journalism."

Millwright hated that the photos were in circulation, but removing them would cause more problems than it solved. The offender had been assigned to spider pit maintenance, then organics disposal.

Like Goldilocks, Millwright required something in between. Captain Irving was one such resource. The new captain was intelligent, believed in the DRI's mission, and held his other morals loosely. Millwright suspected that Charlie Morrissey might be similarly flexible since he had struck up a friendship with a vigilante. The prior relationship with a MEC could prove problematic, but the woman had jilted him, which might work in the DRI's favor.

Millwright would keep Morrissey out of the zoo until his loyalties had settled. That was all he could do for the time being.

Millwright crossed the room, carefully took down the oil painting, and flicked the light switch beside the wide pane of glass hidden behind it. The illumination brought the tiny room's occupant to his feet in a flash.

Percy Rawlings soundlessly pounded on the glass. A steak lay untouched on a plate in the corner. Millwright wondered how long his brother would hold out before he climbed down from his high horse and ate meat. So far, it had been seventy-two hours.

Millwright pressed another button, and Percy's voice exploded from a speaker.

"*You bastard!* I'd feed you to a lion, but lions deserve

better. I will *destroy* you. You won't escape the threads of fate. I will wrap them around your miserable neck and *pull*."

"Is that any way to greet your little brother? No heart-warming family reunion?"

The king cobra, which had slipped off its post when Millwright removed the painting, streaked across the room and struck the glass, fangs bared.

Hope twinkled in his captive brother's eyes. Percy ceased his pounding and knelt to make eye contact with the cobra. "Prickles, it's me. It's okay, buddy."

The snake did not stop its furious attacks, even when Percy laid his hand on the glass.

Millwright could not stand his brother's Dr. Doolittle schtick. He allowed the cobra to continue for half a minute to drive the point home. Animals had to be governed with an iron fist. Percy's coddling would win him no friends of any species down here.

He flicked his fingers, and the snake slithered away. In the enclosure, Percy began to cry. Malcolm's upper lip curled, and he turned off the light to hide the pathetic sniveling.

Millwright's mind teemed with plans. Percy would be much more entertaining than any of the tank's previous occupants. The three most recent had been a boa constrictor, an orangutan, and a cave spider. None had lasted long enough for real fun. He suspected his blubbering brother would prove similarly weak.

Millwright rhythmically twisted his eggplant-colored bowtie and hoped Percy would prove him wrong.

CHAPTER NINE

Birdsong twittered through the forest, so Ellis believed she had a chance. She waited a moment, then clapped three times again. Flower barked supportively.

Ilva frowned. "Are you quite well?"

Errol snorted. Ellis glared at him, daring him to comment, then stared into the forest. If no animals answered her call, it would not matter if they thought she was crazy.

A small raccoon marched to the rotting end of a downed log that protruded into the clearing, and a crow landed on a nearby branch. The black-masked creature chittered softly in Flower's direction.

"Hello," Ellis murmured.

Claire sharply inhaled and asked Ilva, "Is this another of your 'skills?'"

Ellis was surprised to see recognition on her mother's face rather than shock or amazement. That was curious.

"No. The drow cannot speak to animals." Ilva was as curious as Claire.

Ellis rolled her eyes. "Anyone can speak to animals. Getting them to reply is the hard part."

Ellis broke her tunnel bar into several pieces, then ate one and tossed the rest to the animals. As she chewed, she considered her options. The crow's flight would outstrip humans' walking speed. Whoever was tracking the drone might grow suspicious.

She knelt by the raccoon and offered it the tracker. "I need you to take this away from us. A few miles would be great, but if anyone gets close to you, drop it and hide."

"Where's its collar?" Claire was confused.

Ellis raised an eyebrow. She did not understand the question.

"The only way to control an animal outside of captivity is a shock collar," Claire explained.

"Don't let Percy hear you say that," Ellis muttered.

The thought of Percy being imprisoned in the DRI complex brought her back to the task at hand. "Do you understand what I want?" she asked the raccoon.

It hesitated and eyed Flower.

"Play dead," Ellis told the dog.

Flower collapsed and rolled onto her back, exposing her silky belly. Her wagging tail swept over the dirt.

The raccoon snatched the tracker and disappeared into the forest. The crow cocked its head as though expecting orders, and Ellis gently shooed it away. She would not risk any more animals.

"Thank you," she told it. "Enjoy the snack."

Ilva tilted her head. "Why not destroy the tracker?"

Ellis straightened and brushed off the knees of her jeans. "Then the DRI would start their search here, and they might track us. If we can convince them we went somewhere else, they'll be much easier to avoid."

Ilva nodded. "A reasonable plan. I do not understand your connection to that animal, but there is no time to lose."

Claire's knee popped as she stood, and she winced in pain. Ilva was unsympathetic to Claire's aging joints. "Move, human."

"Give her a tunnel bar," Ellis suggested.

The drow woman considered it, then shook her head. "I will not divert precious resources to our enemy."

"She's not our enemy! She's my *mom*."

Ilva was half-hidden by trees. "One does not preclude the other."

They traveled for a few hours, slowed by Claire's knees and her inability to see in the dark. Finally, Ilva stopped at the foot of an oak tree. "We will camp here."

Claire leaned against the tree trunk and shivered, and then slid down it and hugged her knees. "Can we light a fire?"

Ilva shook her head. "It will neither rain nor freeze tonight. You will survive."

Flower noticed Ellis' worried face and sidled up to Claire, offering warmth. Humans preferred warmer temperatures than the cave-dwelling drow.

Ellis hunkered down and crossed her legs. "What's your plan? Where are we going?"

Frustration cracked Ilva's smooth façade. "I do not know," she finally admitted. "I did not plan for this many enemy encounters. I must think through our next steps carefully. I will take the first watch. Errol will take the second."

Ellis scowled. "You trust *him* more than me? One of us has worked for the DRI recently, and it isn't me."

Ilva pursed her lips. "Then I will take both watches. You will rise at dawn."

"Don't be ridiculous. You're exhausted. If you try to stay up all night, you'll pass out."

The older woman's eyes were dull with fatigue. Her sigh told of deep irritation with her mortal weakness. "Fine. I will wake you for the second watch."

Ellis dreamed about her escape from the DRI complex via the service tunnel. In her dream, the shaft got longer with every rung she climbed, and the spiders' eyes glittered and their mandibles clicked as they approached. The rungs were ice-cold, and Ellis' hands stiffened until she slipped and fell toward the writhing mass of arachnids.

Warmth pierced the cold terror as Claire grabbed Ellis' arm and pulled her to safety. Her smile was beatific, and light shone at the end of the tunnel above.

Ilva's face, not Claire's, greeted her when she woke. The older drow woman looked even more haunted than when Ellis had fallen asleep. Ilva's reluctant gaze hung on her for a long time before she curled up on her side near Errol.

Half an hour into her watch, Ellis considered her options. If not for Ilva's stubbornness, she would have been sleeping in her bed at the homestead, working with her father on a plan to rescue Landon. Surely, *he* would understand that Claire was not the enemy.

The warmth from her dream lingered. When she looked at her sleeping mother, Flower curled at her back, it intensified. Claire might not be perfect, but she *had* saved Ellis' life. She deserved better than an endless cold march through the forest.

The dark trees swirled into a formless slate-green mass. Ellis allowed her gaze to wander. She would hear trouble before she saw it.

Her homesickness grew like an itch. The more she ignored it, the more it burned. The longer they spent in this limbo, the harder it would be to find Landon.

Ilva was old-school. She was afraid of outsiders to the point of paranoia. She had backed them into an endless open plain, and she might be too stubborn to retreat.

Cautiously, Ellis placed a hand on her mother's shoulder, then covered Claire's mouth with her hand as she jolted awake. Ellis raised a finger to her lips, and Claire nodded. Flower, now also awake, sat up.

They crept out of the camp slowly, but they had no choice. If Ilva woke up, she would stop them, possibly with arrows, so silence trumped speed. Step by tiny step, they escaped, leaving Ilva and Errol asleep behind them.

When they were well into the forest, Claire quietly asked, "Where are we going?"

It was too late to turn back. Ellis let out her breath in a long hiss. "You helped me. It's my turn to help you."

CHAPTER TEN

"I wish the tunnel I built for Granny was still open," Ellis muttered. She trusted Claire, but taking her to the homestead's main entrance would be unwise after Ilva's reaction.

Claire gasped. "You know your grandmother?"

"Yeah, but she's dead."

"What?"

Ellis frowned, not understanding the alarm on Claire's face. "She died when I was nine."

"Oh. Connor's mother." Claire packed so much longing in the way she said "Connor" that Ellis was embarrassed for her.

"Granny's the name of my Harley," Ellis explained.

"Ah." Claire pushed prickly-needled branches aside and followed Ellis over a fallen tree. "You know, your other grandmother's still alive. My mom."

Ellis tripped over a rock, which she would swear had materialized out of thin air. She hit the ground and let out an *oof.* She was having trouble parsing this revelation. She had been so desperate to find Claire that she had not considered the existence of other relatives.

"Does she live in Los Angeles?"

Claire winced. "Sorry. The last time we spoke, she was in Florida."

"When was that?"

"Ten years ago, when Dad died," Claire softly confessed.

Anger and confusion bubbled up inside Ellis. "Why don't you talk to her?"

"It's complicated."

"Yeah, well, *my* life was complicated, but if I'd found you, I wouldn't be so ungrateful. I wouldn't cut you out. Not even…" *If you sold me out to an evil lab?* "Not even if I was angry."

"Yes, well, *maybe* after you've known me for longer than *two days*, you'll understand." Claire sat heavily on a nearby rock and turned away when Ellis approached. "I need a break."

She retreated into herself. Ellis was unable to prod Claire into further conversation, so she sat cross-legged on the forest floor and planned until Claire deigned to move again.

The drow had caved in her secret tunnel, but it had not been the homestead's only remote access point. Ellis gave the drow rangers' typical territory a wide berth and headed for a crevice below a fallen log on a nondescript hillside. She was lucky that she had gotten her bearings enough to recognize the secret entrance.

Ellis crawled in first, followed by her mother. Flower brought up the rear. The first ten feet were not pleasant.

Ellis' heart rate spiked as crumbling wood and soil brushed her sides and back, but the tight squeeze was over before she panicked. The rough entrance opened into a clean rock shaft with handholds chipped into the sides.

Ellis started down but paused when her mother made an uncomfortable sound.

"I'm not sure I can do this," Claire admitted nervously.

"It isn't far," Ellis reassured her. "I'll catch you if you fall."

She was unsure if she could catch her mother *and* keep a grip on the ladder, but she hoped the reassurance would raise her mother's confidence enough that they would not have to find out.

Claire might doubt her abilities, but Flower could *not* make the descent. She barked twice, and the noise echoed off the walls. Ellis contemplated turning her shirt into a sling but could not return to the homestead half-naked.

"I'll come back for you, girl," Ellis called. "Stay out of sight for now."

Flower responded with a cheerful bark, then disappeared. Ellis heard the click of her nails on the stone, then a *huff* as the dog settled in to wait.

The descent was challenging but not grueling. Soon, the two women stood at the entrance to a tall, narrow tunnel with an arched ceiling.

Claire's blue eyes reflected the amber light of the bioluminescent lichen that clung to the magically hewn rock. The woman was engaged in a way Ellis had not seen before, not even she had met Ellis.

Don't take it personally. A lot was happening.

"What is it?" Ellis inquired.

"I never thought I would make it down here," Claire told her. "I gave up on this dream a long time ago."

Ellis squeezed her mother's hand. Claire started but smiled when Ellis replied, "Here we are. Let's find Dad."

Ellis had chosen one of the homestead's most remote entrances, so they faced a long walk. Claire trailed her fingers along the smooth rock, then paused to inspect an outcrop of tiny mushrooms in a crack. The mushrooms were common pearlcaps, but Claire touched them with wonder.

"What do they grow on?"

"Some cracks house a substance we call rock rust. Small mushrooms can live on it."

"What is it?"

Ellis realized she did not know, and that embarrassed her. "Just part of the landscape."

"Maybe geomicrobes," Claire mused. She plunged a finger into the crack, then dug it out and examined the rusty powder on the pad of her finger.

Happiness surged in Ellis. She could finally share her childhood. She would show her mother the mushroom caverns and the strains Ellis had carefully cultivated. She would show her the crystal caverns in which she had played, the Great Hall, the infirmary where her father had taught her to make potions...

Claire followed the line of pearlcaps toward a recessed alcove. Inside, bright chartreuse mushrooms with white inclusions sprouted from the walls and floor. Ellis drew a blank on the name of the species.

They had to keep moving. Ellis was forced to drag

Claire away from her mycological explorations. "If we drag our feet, Ilva might catch up," she told Claire. That resulted in a significant increase in speed.

They turned a corner and came face to face with a drow ranger lounging in a short connecting passage. He was cleaning his fingernails with the tip of his dagger. Ellis' appearance startled him, and he shot to his feet.

It was Rollo. His skin was the dark blue of the deep ocean, and his ash-gray hair swooped across his face. He had probably expected tunnel duty to be a bore. Ellis knew him only in passing—he was several years older than her, so their paths rarely crossed—but he had never gone out of his way to be cruel to her.

That did not stop him from panicking and raising his dagger when he spotted Claire.

Ellis held up her hands. "It's okay. She's a friend."

That did not appease him. He reached for the floor, presumably gathering shadow magic, then fanned his fingers and pointed above Ellis' and Claire's heads.

Ellis protested, but it was too late. Rollo had cast a ruin-web. The shadow spell sent thin lances of magic into the rock to destabilize it enough to cause a cave-in.

The rock rumbled, and dirt and pebbles rained on the women as they stumbled forward. Claire screamed, and Ellis looked back in horror to find her mother on the ground with a rock the size of a loaf of bread on her bloody ankle.

Two cracks spread in the ceiling. She could be crushed. Claire crawled away when she saw the danger, but she was hobbled by pain.

Ellis dashed back, grabbed her mother's hand, and

yanked her to safety with every ounce of her strength. The tunnel caved in behind them.

The thick haze blinded Ellis. When it settled, her mother was alive. Injured, yes, and coughing up a storm, but she was breathing. That was better than being flattened into vellum by several tons of rock.

Alas, broken bones were not the worst of their problems. Any drow working nearby would have heard the cave-in and raised the alarm.

"You idiot! This is my mother!" Ellis shouted at Rollo. She crouched beside Claire to offer comfort. Once, she could have done something to help, but no longer. Claire's skin was cold when she touched it. Sweat beaded on it like ice water beaded a glass.

Rollo defensively raised his dagger. His other hand curled, doubtless collecting shadow magic. "If you move a silk thread's width closer to the homestead, I *will* obliterate you."

Adrenaline made her head ache. All Ellis could do was nod.

Shadow magic could cut through rock, so it easily cut through people. It was taboo to use in that way except under extreme circumstances like existential threats to the homestead. This hardly qualified, but Rollo's expression face suggested that he thought it did.

Claire's breathing was ragged. "She needs an infirmarian," Ellis told him.

"If you come closer, she will need *many* infirmarians."

They remained in a standoff for several minutes before footsteps echoed down the corridor. Connor Burton arrived and pushed past Rollo.

"Sir—" Rollo began, but Connor did not stop.

"Ellis! You're safe!" He wrapped her in a worried embrace. Ellis hugged him back. Then he went still.

Claire laughed breathlessly and painfully. "Hello, Con."

CHAPTER ELEVEN

Ellis' father released her. The only sounds in the tunnel were the shouts of the drow elders who had followed Connor.

Ellis had not allowed herself to consider her parents' reunion. She had focused on the journey and their previous relationship rather than her father's reaction.

He clenched his hands to stop their trembling. Torment pooled in his eyes, which were as cold and dark as an ice crust on a deep-cavern pool. "What have you *done?*"

Rollo reluctantly spoke up. "Should I kill the intruder, sir?"

Panic shot through Ellis. She leaped at Rollo with a scream, and he reflexively slashed at her. Her rash attack had left her vulnerable. His blade would connect with her throat, and she could do nothing about it.

She let out a strangled shriek as the cold steel connected with her windpipe. Ellis closed her eyes and waited for the sharp pain to fade into terminal darkness.

Then the ache faded. Ellis opened her eyes in confusion and found Rollo staring, open-mouthed, at the hilt of his dagger. The blade had dissolved.

Ellis touched her neck, and her fingers came away dry. Her father had saved her life. She opened her mouth to thank him but stopped when she saw the fury and fear in his face.

Connor nodded at Claire. "Take her to a cell. Don't harm her unless she tries to escape."

"She's in shock," Ellis told him. "Her foot…"

"Be *quiet!*" Connor snapped.

Ellis' jaw dropped. She had never seen her father this angry. His ire had turned his pale-lavender skin ruddy.

He spoke to Rollo. "Check her for weapons. Send an infirmarian to visit, but ensure that no one speaks to her alone."

Rollo nodded and tugged Claire to her feet. She swayed, and her eyes glazed over with pain. Some drow showed up with a stretcher, and Rollo lifted Claire onto it.

Ellis tried to follow her half-conscious mother, but her father held her back. "I'm going with her," she protested.

"You are *not.*" Connor's voice was as hard as a diamond. When Ellis tried to push past him, he grabbed her arm and held fast.

Another ranger was looking at Ellis with the trepidation with which he would regard a cave spider. "Should we restrain her too, sir?"

Connor shook his head. "I will take responsibility for Ellis. Leave a brigade to guard the outsider and call the homestead to the Great Hall."

The ranger fidgeted. "Sorry, sir, but who? The elders?"

"*Everyone.*"

Connor did not give Ellis an opportunity to act before he strode past the rangers with her in tow. Her attempts to wriggle away were futile.

At length, he asked her, "Where's Landon?"

"Kidnapped," she replied. "That's why I came to—"

He cut her off. "By Claire's people?"

"They're not 'her people' anymore."

Her father's reply was a snarl. "Is *that* what she told you?"

Ellis tried again to dig her heels in and slow him down. It was no use. "Dad, *stop!*"

"No time. We must protect the homestead from invasion."

"What are you *talking* about? There will be no *invasion.* She wanted to help us find Landon."

Connor hissed. "You cannot judge your mother by her honeyed words. You have trusted her, and the Swallow's Nest will pay the price."

Her father's words made no sense. Claire had come here for Landon's sake, not as part of a nefarious plan.

Embarrassment curled in Ellis' gut. In her daydreams about sharing her childhood with her mother, she had not considered that other drow might be present, let alone her father. She realized how short-sighted that had been.

Connor shot her a glare. "What did I tell you about the DRI's symbol?"

"You told me to run if I saw it, but I don't run away from problems." She blinked. "Wait. You know about the DRI?"

Connor stopped pulling Ellis and turned to face her. Even in the low light of the tunnels, Connor's face got ruddier. A drow couple emerged from a nearby room and stopped dead.

"What's going on?" the woman asked.

"Good question," Ellis muttered.

Connor gestured down the passage. "All-meet in the Great Hall. Now."

The man looked affronted. "An all-meet? About what?" His partner shushed him and pulled him away.

When the couple disappeared around the corner, Ellis demanded, "If you hate humans so much, why did you have me?"

Connor's grip on her arm loosened. "I do not hate humans."

"Yes, you do. I can see it in your face."

"I do not hate humans in general. My hatred for the DRI was well-earned." Connor sighed. Shame pulled at the corners of his lips. "I tried to be a good father despite everything. My failure to earn your trust is my greatest shortcoming."

"You *did* earn my trust," Ellis protested. "I admit that I meddled with the DRI when I shouldn't have, but what does that have to do with Mom?"

"She is not your mother!" he snapped.

Ellis glared. "She *could* have been if you hadn't kept me a prisoner here for so long! And now, when I *finally* meet her, the first thing you do is imprison her."

"The DRI is an existential threat to the drow," Connor insisted.

"She hasn't worked for them in years," Ellis argued.

"Was that what she told you?"

"It's the truth."

"It is not. Your mother never left the DRI."

The words hit Ellis like a gut punch, but she crossed her arms in an attempt to keep her cool. "How would you know? You cower in these tunnels and refuse to leave your precious hidey-hole." It was a low blow, but Ellis was not feeling charitable.

Connor's mouth set in a thin line. "I am not as much of a hermit as you imagine. I am merely cautious about my interactions with the outside world, and deservedly so."

Ellis remembered the drow-stonework table in the cabin. She might not know everything about the drow, but her father could not be right about this. "If my mother was still working for the DRI, she wouldn't have helped me escape," Ellis stated firmly.

Connor raised an eyebrow. His grim expression shifted to grudging appreciation. "So, she won your loyalty by freeing you after she locked you up? Was that how she convinced you to reveal our location?"

Doubt roiled in Ellis' mind. What had Claire said when she had entered the homestead? Not, "I've always wanted to see where you grew up," but "I never thought I would make it down here."

If Ellis allowed herself to consider the possibility that Claire had liberated her as part of a twisted plot, she might throw up. Claire had insisted on seeing Connor, but on reflection, they could have met on the surface. She gripped the sleeve of her father's robe and swallowed hard. "You can't. I'm only just getting to know her."

The fear and anger on Connor's face became bittersweet sorrow, and he wrapped Ellis in his arms. "I was so afraid for you and Landon," he whispered.

Ellis hugged him. Her father's fears about their relationship were unfounded. She did trust him, even though he pissed her off.

"I'm scared for him, too. That was why I brought her here," Ellis weakly explained.

Connor held Ellis at arm's length and watched the emotions swirling on her face. Finally, he sighed again. "I had hoped to keep many things from you, but the past has caught up with me. I will tell you everything later. Now, we must act."

He released her and strode down the tunnel. She followed, and when the tunnel met a broad corridor, they joined a river of drow heading for the Great Hall. It felt like a current bearing them toward a waterfall. Having horrible happen was inevitable.

The drow regarded Ellis with their customary suspicion when they thought she could not see them. She ignored them, and they averted their eyes when Connor frowned at them. When a hand caught her shoulder, Ellis spun and brought up her fists.

Trissa shied away. She was Landon's girlfriend and had, however briefly, cured Ellis' lack of shadow magic.

Ellis stopped dead. Two drow slammed into her back and muttered curses before shoving past. The river of people broke around them.

Trissa's face was pinched, and green circles of exhaustion sagged under her eyes. "Have you brought word of Landon?"

Ellis' heart sank. "No one talked to you? I thought Ilva

had." Her father could not be relied upon to provide timely, relevant information, but Ilva was different.

Trissa shook her head. They were close to the infirmary, so Ellis took Trissa's arm and moved in that direction.

"We should go to the all-meet," Trissa protested.

"We have time. It'll take some of the elders an hour to climb the stairs."

When they were ensconced in the quiet, empty infirmary, Ellis dropped down on the first cot, leaned against the wall, and let out a heavy sigh.

"Are you all right?" Trissa's question was professional, not empathetic.

Ellis considered her response. If she asked the woman for more of the shadow magic potion, she could get her magic back. The last time she had used it, she had blown up a wide swath of forest, but this time, she would not drink as much. A sip, maybe a gulp, and she could save Landon...except that he was trapped in a basement stuffed to the gills with lightsilk.

"Landon was taken," Ellis stated flatly.

Trissa's eyes widened. "Taken? By who, the official who tried to detain us at the music gathering? How would he have—"

Ellis interrupted her. "No, not Charlie. Charlie is..." The word "trustworthy" died on her lips. He had been, but then he had betrayed her and Percy. He had also turned on Percy's cobra, but Ellis could not blame the man for that.

Had the DRI welcomed Charlie with open arms, or had they been suspicious? The DRI had a track record of cold-blooded murder. She doubted they were making friendship bracelets even though Charlie and Liza knew each other.

The cold realization that Charlie might be in as much trouble as Percy curdled in her heart. The infirmary's low ceilings, meant to be comforting, loomed.

Trissa was expectantly staring at her. Ellis rubbed her temples and continued. "There's a military organization with an underground facility in Los Angeles…"

Trissa listened intently as Ellis explained what she could. Her questions were intelligent, but despite her visits to Los Angeles, there were wide lacunae in her knowledge about the human world. Ellis felt for her. Ellis still had blank spots, even after years.

When Ellis finished her explanation, the bags under Trissa's eyes were even greener. Her relationship with Landon was no fling.

Ellis bit her lip and took Trissa's hand. "Do you have any more of the potion you made? I still have no magic."

Trissa grimaced. "Shadow magic might not help."

"What do you mean? Of course, it will."

Trissa shook her head. "This organization, the *moon men,* are well-guarded against shadow magic with their lightsilk weapons and cages. Perhaps you should not fight them using the thing they are best equipped to combat. Come. We should attend the all-meet."

Ellis was quiet and thoughtful on the way to the Great Hall. Shadow magic was useful on the drow homestead, and it had made Ellis nearly indestructible in her normal dealings in Los Angeles. She had become accustomed to using it to solve the smallest problems. Maybe she needed to think outside the box.

The halls were now empty. Ellis entertained a brief daydream about rescuing her mother from drow detention. She imagined slipping past the guards and heroically pulling Claire to safety.

Where would they go afterward? The rangers would have doubled or even tripled their patrols, and although she loathed admitting it, her father's words had nurtured the seed of doubt that had been planted the moment her mother had ripped off her helmet in the park. Ellis wanted to hear what Connor had to say, and if she acted rashly, she might lose that chance.

The terraced cavern was packed with worried purple faces. Ellis had intended to rejoin her father, but he was on the top tier, and she would not be able to reach him without causing a scene. Even now, the crowd shied away from Ellis' mushroom-cap skin. Thankfully, Trissa slid into the gap.

They shifted uncomfortably until the low hum of a singing bowl on the highest tier pierced the crowd's murmurings. The drow musician let the ringing fade to silence.

Beside him, an elderly drow woman named Katya banged a metal staff on the stone floor. She was at least a hundred and fifty years old and still panting from the climb up the sixteen terraces. Her long, dark robes were intricately embroidered with cool colors, indicating that she was the current Elder Speaker. The wrinkles on her dark blue face were like deep sea trenches, but her voice was clear and rich.

"At the call of Connor Burton, we have gathered under

one ceiling. By shadow and stone, speak." She banged the staff again, then offered it to Connor.

Ellis' father was a steady and decisive person. He was as solid as the stone in which they lived. That being said, the cave-in that had nearly crushed Claire had shown that even solid rock could crumble under enough stress, and even from this distance, Connor looked as though *he* might be crumbling. His hand trembled as he accepted the staff from Katya.

He sought Ellis in the crowd. Her pale face was easy to find, but his gaze only lingered for a second. "Fellows, friends, family, I will not mince words. Our people have long lived in the shadows. Many have forgotten the sun-touched world above, but it has not forgotten about us. A human has found the homestead."

Her father continued over the murmurs of the assembly. "I have reason to believe that she has led others here. You all heard the alerts, which occurred when we collapsed the tunnel behind her.

"This intruder did not stumble on an entrance by accident. She entered as part of a careful deception."

Ellis tried to ignore the troubled faces turning toward her and the people nearest her inching away lest they be found guilty by association. Connor's words cast Claire as a villain and painted Ellis as a credulous rube.

Trissa's cool hand landed on her arm, and Ellis drew several deep breaths.

The singing bowl droned to life again. When the room was silent, Connor continued. "The tunnel collapse has bought us time but not safety. The humans who wish us ill *will* return with weapons and equipment, so we must act now. I do not speak these next words lightly, but circumstances give me no choice. I call for retreat. I call for a tunnel-out."

The ensuing uproar was so loud that Ellis clapped her hands over her ears.

Trissa put her mouth beside Ellis' ear. "Did you know what he would propose?"

Ellis mutely shook her head. A tunnel-out was the most extreme defense, undertaken only in response to existential threats.

A tunnel-out was a mass migration. Every adult shadow mage, and sometimes the older teens, would work together to build a new tunnel that led away from the incoming danger. When the tunnel was complete, they would collapse the old homestead behind them.

It made the drow impossible to follow, but it required immense amounts of energy and often drastically affected the surrounding environment. The 1906 San Francisco earthquake had been caused by a drow nest in Northern California tunneling out after being disrupted by a mining operation.

When the drow population was smaller and contact with humans more frequent, tunnel-outs had happened often. Nowadays, underground activity was more difficult to conceal from modern technology.

Connor Burton had called the DRI an existential threat. Ellis had thought he was using hyperbole to make her feel guilty, but he had been serious. Helpless laughter threatened to bubble out of her as her dream of showing her mother the mushroom caverns caved in.

Ellis remembered the map she had found in her mother's belongings. The approximate area of the homestead had been circled on it.

An image of lightsilk-clad soldiers marauding through the tunnels, draining drow magic and answering arrows with bullets, filled her mind's eye. *If the DRI invaded the homestead, they could wipe us out.*

Five minutes passed before the drone of the singing bowl overcame the din. The crowd was reluctant to agree with her father.

"Humans are weak," a drow elder argued. "We don't need to tunnel out."

"They are not as weak as we remember," Ellis' father rebutted. "Their weapons and technology are much stronger."

"We need not fear their toys. The shadows protect us!" another drow cried.

"For a long time, that was true," Connor agreed, "but these humans have lightsilk."

This pronouncement did not induce another outcry but a lengthy silence. Grim faces accused Ellis, but she had earned the dirty looks they directed at her.

"How did the humans obtain lightsilk?" the first drow elder asked.

Connor waited a long time before replying. When he did, his gaze touched Ellis again. "They have lightsilk because I gave it to them."

Trissa gasped. Ellis' blood ran cold.

Her father gripped the staff. "I will face whatever consequences the elders deem just, but my past sins do not erase our current danger. I believe we are capable of meeting this challenge. The drow have built new homesteads before and can do so again. The years ahead will be hard, but we will carve a darker future from the stone for ourselves."

"How can we trust you?" someone shouted.

"What if he's leading us into greater danger?" someone else asked.

The chatter increased. Ellis kept hearing one word: "Traitor." The ugly looks cast in her direction were more pointed. The drow were eager to pour their anger, fear, and confusion into violence, and the only "human" they had to attack was her.

Trissa tugged Ellis' sleeve and pointed. On the lowest terrace, three young drow had unsheathed their daggers and were moving toward Trissa and Ellis. The assembly allowed them to pass. Some moved out of fear, but others muttered encouragement.

Ellis had no weapons, magic, or protection, so she had only one option.

Ellis ran.

She did not go far. The drow surged around her to prevent her escape. Trissa clenched her fists and interposed herself between Ellis and the others. "Go!"

The Great Hall was lit by phosphorescent mushrooms, but little of that light reached the floor with so many drow packed in. Trissa took full advantage of the darkness and pulled cantaloupe-sized balls of shadow magic into her open palms.

The drow skittered aside, allowing Ellis a view of the long tables that lined the perimeter of each terrace. She dove between two drow, rolled, and leaped onto a table.

The staircase that led up the terraces was choked with

people. Ellis ran across the tables, searching for an opening and wishing Ilva had not taken her grapnel.

She spied a gap in the crowd and prepared to jump. Someone grabbed her ankle, and she pitched forward. She managed to roll and hit the table with her shoulder.

The fall bruised bone. Ellis screamed and tried to stand, but drow grabbed her from every side. They lifted her above their heads and passed her forward in a parody of crowd-surfing. The ceiling in that area was so low that she scraped her forehead on it.

As Ellis was brought into the amphitheater, she saw a purple blur streaking down the central staircase. Someone did not move fast enough and was thrown aside.

The blur stopped at the base of the stairs and vaulted over the crowd with the help of a staff. From her position, Ellis saw that it was her father, still carrying the ceremonial staff.

"*Dad!*"

He swept the staff in a low arc and toppled the drow who were carrying her above their heads like bowling pins. Ellis fell with them, but their bodies provided ample cushioning.

Connor pulled her to her feet, and the drow she was standing on let out an "Oof."

"Thanks," Ellis rasped.

"*Silence!*"

The Elder Speaker's voice echoed through the cavern. Connor wrapped his arms around Ellis and said something inaudible.

"*Drow of the Swallow's Nest, I will have* order!" Katya shouted.

Her arms were outstretched, not in supplication but with a black hole's worth of shadow magic. Ellis could see the threads despite her deadened magic. Katya had cast a tricky one-way sound barrier that muffled their voices but allowed them to hear her.

Katya looked ready to beat the DRI to the punch and obliterate the drow herself. "Cease behaving like children and come to *order!*"

The drow Connor had knocked over scrambled upright, although one shoved Ellis.

Katya glared. "Connor Burton has proposed a dire solution for a threat we barely understand. Would anyone else speak?"

Mouths flapped in angry silence until Katya noticed a figure ascending the staircase with her hands raised in supplication. It was Ilva.

Ellis grimaced. She had hoped to have more time before Ilva made it back. The expert ranger must have sensed something wrong and woken up soon after Claire and Ellis had left.

Katya gestured, and Ilva put a hand to her throat in relief.

Ilva's voice was hard and clear. "The honored Connor Burton proposes retreat. He suggests we abandon all we have created and start anew in some Mother-forsaken place where we must scrabble among the rocks for a meager existence.

"On one thing, we agree. Humans pose a dire threat. The woman Ellis brought to the edge of our homestead leads a group of humans who wish to eradicate our people. Instead of retreat, I propose we force the intruder to provide information. We will use that to eliminate the threat. It is time our enemies understood our strength."

Ellis drew a breath. Ilva was proposing torture and a frontal assault. Ellis preferred fight to flight, but she could not allow them to hurt her mother.

Katya spoke next. "Two paths have been proposed: a tunnel-out and an attack. We must not choose rashly. The Council of Elders will convene tomorrow. We will speak to the human intruder and hear more about Ilva's plan. If anyone wishes to present evidence, speak to our clerk, and he will assign an audience time."

Katya moved to bang her staff, but her hand curled around empty air. She glared down at Connor, then flicked her hands and dismissed the silencing spell.

Ellis' heart rate picked up. She had to leave. The drow would turn on her again, and she had to save her mother from torture.

Before she could leave, her father's hand landed on her shoulder. "Ellis."

She pulled away. "Let me go! They'll hurt her."

"The guards I set on your mother are loyal to me. They will not harm her, nor will they allow others to do so. If the council agrees to follow Ilva's plan?" He sighed. "We will find another solution."

Ellis shifted uneasily. If they waited that long, it might be too late.

Her father read her mind. "We have time. The council will not convene for several hours, and they are not known for swift decision-making." That was true. Consensus government moved slower than a cavern slug. "Will you wait, Ellis? Please?"

Ellis stilled. She was used to having her father give orders. A request? That was new. If he could change his spots, so could she. "I will wait until the council convenes." That way, the most powerful shadow mages would be distracted.

Connor eyed her calculatingly. "Good. In that case, it is time we talked."

CHAPTER TWELVE

Charlie still tensed every time he saw someone in DRI fatigues. He kept reminding himself that these were now his coworkers, at least in name. The constant adrenaline spikes exhausted him.

He grumbled. "If I'd stayed in my cozy detention cell, I could have been asleep."

"Buck up, Charlie." Liza's cheerful, familiar tone was comforting. That normalcy, more than the words, raised his spirits.

"I'm not sure what I've gotten myself into."

"You've scored a few more days of living. Alive is better than dead."

Charlie suspected that serving the DRI might be the exception to that.

The facility had quieted. The alarms had been turned off, and the lighting was back to normal. They stopped a pair of soldiers trudging down the hall.

"What's going on?" Liza asked.

"I don't know. They called us off."

"Was the MEC recaptured?"

Morrissey shifted his weight to the balls of his feet. Had Ellis escaped? A pit opened in his stomach when it struck him that she might have been killed in the escape attempt.

"It's not in the cages, and my buddy at the lab says it didn't come in dead."

"What didn't?" Charlie interjected.

Liza waved apologetically. "He's new. They're talking about the MEC, Charlie."

"You mean El—"

Liza elbowed him *hard*, and he coughed. The jab nauseated him. They were talking about Ellis like she was an object, not a person.

Liza finished the exchange of small talk, then pulled Charlie down the corridor.

"What are we doing now? Insurance paperwork? Contract? Is this a ruse that ends with you chucking me into the organics disposal shaft?"

Liza leveled a glower at him. "We're going to *Requisitions*, ass. I'm not sure the director plans to keep you, but I can kit you out."

"Can I have my gun back?"

Liza snorted, then paused in front of a door. "First thing you need to know is door protocol. It's simple. Doors stay closed *at all times*. MECs can turn invisible, so you open them *just* enough to walk through. *Never* prop them open, even if you'll only be gone for a few seconds. If you wear your silks, they have to keep their distance."

Charlie remembered practicing that with Ellis. He could silently lead her through a building while she followed at his heels.

"When you say silks, do you mean…" He stopped before he said lightsilk. He decided he did not want Liza to understand the extent of his knowledge yet.

"The material you see the soldiers wearing. It repels MECs."

"How?"

Liza made a face. "As far as I can tell, they don't know. The materials lab made improvements to the fabric through guesswork, but apparently, it's difficult to study."

She pointed at the door. Now that he was paying attention, it was smaller than a typical door. The architectural change made sense, given the door protocol, but it felt claustrophobic.

He felt ridiculous going through the door as Liza watched him, as though he were a toddler learning to tie his shoes. If she had any critiques of his technique, however, she kept them to herself as she slipped in behind him.

Automatic lighting flicked on as they entered a warehouse-type space, which reminded Charlie of the evidence locker. He eyed the unmanned reception desk, which was covered in clutter and dust. "Are we supposed to talk to someone?"

"No. The DRI is understaffed. The funding comes from a classified section of the federal military budget, but it's hard to keep the higher-ups invested in something no one is allowed to know about. Who wants to fund a budget line that effectively says, 'Trust me?' Not to mention, Director Millwright is…"

Charlie kept his body language neutral as he waited for Liza to finish the sentence.

She rolled her eyes. *"Difficult."*

Charlie snorted. "Really? He seemed so nice and easygoing."

"Yeah, yeah. He creeps me out, too. The animal lab is a separate personal project that I don't want to ask about. Play nice, okay? Staffing shortages means he's incentivized to keep you, particularly with the senator visiting."

That was curious. "Senator?"

"She's on the Senate Committee on Armed Services. They sent her to California to hunt down 'military bloat.' Part of me thinks Millwright is crazy to hire you with such a sensitive moment approaching."

Morrissey raised an eyebrow.

She scoffed. "You know what I mean. You want seasoned personnel in situations like these, but this place is so understaffed that he's jumping on every opportunity to beef up his numbers even if it might blow up in his face."

"When is the senator coming?"

"In a couple days. Don't be surprised if they put you to work cleaning bathrooms."

"Anything for my country."

Cleaning bathrooms would give him time to think and explore. The senator's visit was an opportunity. Everyone would be on their best behavior, even the director, and that kind of pressure revealed cracks. He would break this place open.

CHAPTER THIRTEEN

Her mushroom tea had gone cold. Connor had said nothing meaningful but had insisted on treating Ellis' injuries. When only minor scrapes were left, she pushed him away.

"Dad, you've been stalling for over twenty years. Enough."

"I suppose you're right." He sighed and fiddled with the cloth he had used to dab paste on her bruises. "Please understand that this might be difficult to hear. Those events were among the most challenging of my life."

"*Dad.*"

He huffed. "Very well. I met your mother at a dance."

"She told me it was a rave."

He waved a hand. "My human vocabulary is out of date. You know your grandmother advocated for more contact with the outside world, I trust?"

"Yes. I miss her."

"As do I. Her perspective was not widely accepted, but I

believed in her and decided to explore the human world. I met Claire's friends first."

"Rose?"

Connor looked surprised and nodded while Ellis held back laughter. Her father had been so conservative throughout her childhood that it was hard to imagine a version of him who had willingly met that woman. Maybe they were more alike than she realized.

He cleared his throat and went on. "This was before we had shape-changing medallions. Things might have turned out differently if I had."

Connor recounted his meeting with Claire. Every detail matched her mother's story, but his smile was pained, where hers had been affectionate. *Why so grim, Dad?*

Her father averted his eyes, and his expression darkened as he went on to the next part of the story. "Claire worked as a medical researcher at a facility in the San Fernando Valley when she wasn't seeing patients at the clinic. One night, she took me to her lab.

"I thought she meant to show me a new aspect of Los Angeles and the human experience, but she had other motivations. I believe her motivations changed when she learned my age, but I was so enamored with her that I refused to listen to my instincts."

The hair on the back of Ellis' neck lifted. Connor's words were painfully familiar.

"I loved your mother, Ellis, and that made what happened so much worse. I allowed her to take a sample of my blood."

His voice was bitter and weary. "Humans live short lives.

I was a healer too, and I told myself I was making a positive contribution by allowing her to study me. She made many requests. At first, they were small, for more blood samples and hearing tests, but gradually, they got more invasive.

"The lab visits soon became more frequent than our other encounters. I felt more like a subject than a romantic partner. The situation worsened when her colleague, Dr. Malcolm Millwright, discovered us."

Connor said the name as though the man was a deadly mushroom.

"Millwright had noticed supplies going missing and decided to investigate. He claimed he was looking out for the research institute's bottom line, but I think he wanted secrets that he could use for personal gain. He threatened to report her unless she explained herself."

"Was he a doctor?"

"He was a healer of animals."

"A veterinarian."

"Yes, that is the term." He grimaced. "Although 'healer' is incorrect. Claire claimed he was a genius, but the animals shied away when he walked past their cages. In any case, he immediately took ownership of the research project."

Connor paused and poured more mushroom tea. Ellis' patience was so thin after two decades of waiting for answers that it was transparent. "What research project?" she demanded.

Her father sipped his tea. His grip on the cup was tight. "He claimed he was better positioned to study me because he had studied many species and therefore had a wider base of knowledge. Since Claire only understood humans, she might make incorrect assumptions."

The memory of the pellets' taste filled Ellis' mouth. She gulped her tea. Its chill was a balm for her rising anger. "He was implying that you were more animal than human."

Connor nodded. "Millwright was making a moral claim, but your mother took it as a practical argument since the research project was so important to her. I ignored my reservations because she was important to me.

"We stopped visiting new places. Instead of eating human cuisine together in the Hollywood hills, she gave me bottles of powdered nutrient mixes so she could study my digestion. Eventually, we stopped driving around the city and only went to the lab.

"By then, Millwright was always with her. She assured me that she only needed one more sample or test, but her questions got more aggressive and less curious. She was no longer interested in me as a person or my emotions. Millwright stopped speaking to me at all. I soon sympathized with the lab rats."

Ellis cradled her teacup. Could Claire be that cold? Rose and the other women had described her as warm and deeply dedicated to caring for others. "Maybe she truly did want to help people. She took the Hippocratic oath seriously."

"'First, do no harm,'" her father murmured, then slumped in his chair. "I do not doubt your mother's commitment to the betterment of humanity, but I came to doubt whether I was included."

Ellis had *never* seen her father slump. Embarrassment flooded her. She felt as though she was baking in the sun.

Connor's stonewalling her questions about her mother had seemed like a personal attack. She had not considered that those walls might have been erected to protect himself.

Connor stared at his tea. "I was so foolish. The research project was a warning sign, but I initially considered it a hurdle to overcome. I threw myself ears-first into the testing, believing that the more I did and the quicker I acted, the sooner Claire would be satisfied and all would return to normal.

"I should have guarded our secrets, but I shared them all. I showed Claire my shadow magic, hoping my trust would bring us closer, but it alarmed her. I told her about lightsilk, and she asked for a piece. Millwright didn't ask but *demanded*. That made me uncomfortable, and I refused. Claire did not speak of it again.

"Several weeks later, she brought human food to the lab for the first time in months. Have you had burritos?" He overpronounced the word.

Ellis grinned. "Yeah, Dad, I've eaten burritos. I can't believe *you* have."

Connor smiled sadly. "Chicken with extra guacamole. It's strange, the small details we remember.

"That day, Claire was quiet. She told me she had encountered another drow. She could not describe him, only say that he was purple."

Ellis snorted, and her father's eyebrows twitched in amusement.

"She claimed he had appeared at her apartment and threatened her. She asked if there was any way to protect herself. So, a few days later…"

"You brought her the lightsilk blanket," Ellis finished. The blanket Ron Jackson had acquired.

"I didn't question her story at the time."

"But you do now."

Connor nodded. "I now believe her story was a fiction to obtain what she wanted. I do not blame you for bringing her here. Your mother is very persuasive."

"It's not the same! I'm her *daughter!*" Ellis protested. "She killed people to help me escape." Ellis wondered if the Hippocratic Oath applied to rescuing your kidnapped daughter but decided it was better not to know. "I can accept that she made mistakes, but she stopped working for the DRI."

"She lied to you."

Ellis' face burned. She refused to believe it. Connor's and Claire's relationship had soured, and Connor was upset and wanted to believe the worst. "I was mean when I said this earlier, but it's still valid. How would you know? You never leave the homestead."

Connor did not rise to the bait. "I understand this is difficult for you to believe, but you still do not know the full tale. The location of the Swallow's Nest was the only piece of information I did not divulge. That infuriated Claire."

What if Claire's claim of ignorance regarding the tracker Ilva had found was false?

"I want to talk to her," Ellis stated.

Connor shook his head. "Let me finish."

Ellis fidgeted and struggled to listen. Her father's emotions turned his voice into a drone. She wanted to tell him to shut up so she could think, but that would hardly be fair after the years she had spent demanding answers.

"One night, Claire picked me up. She no longer asked me where I wanted to go. It was always the lab. The lab, and only *the lab*. I was sick of it. When we arrived, I told her I would not go in. I was done with her research project, and if she did not agree to stop, I was done with her, too.

"She began to cry. I thought she would tell me that she wished to stay together. That she would ask for my forgiveness, and we would forge a different path forward.

"Instead, she begged me for 'just one more blood sample.'" He sighed, and it was as though he had deflated. "In my anger, I told her she should drain me dry because she would never see me again."

Ellis grimaced. A blood sample was quite the parting gift.

"Claire was angry. She had believed we were quarreling, but I had told her we were finished. She stormed off, and Millwright approached. He said he understood and offered me a ride home. Said it was the least he could do.

"I should not have accepted, but I was tens of miles from the homestead. It was high summer, and the sun rose early. I was not the mage then that I have since become. I didn't want to be in the open.

"Millwright was unusually friendly. He took a wrong turn, and when I expressed concern, he claimed he had forgotten his wallet and needed to fetch it to buy gas.

"I was too distraught to question that. When we entered the garage, police officers were waiting. I do not believe they were there in an official capacity. I believe Millwright hired them. They subdued me with lightsilk nets. If I'd had a weapon, I might have been able to escape, but I did not bring my dagger to meetings with your mother."

Ellis nodded. If that was anyone but Ron Jackson and his cronies, she would eat a lightsilk blanket. She was both horrified and relieved. Claire had not kidnapped him. She could not be held responsible for the actions of her research partner.

Connor grimaced. "What happened next was the darkest period of my life. Millwright had constructed a cell using the lightsilk sample Claire had shared. He had increased its potency so that the threads somehow burned. I understand you have encountered it."

Ellis touched the fading scar of a burn on her arm and nodded.

Her father sounded like a dead man. "I was powerless. Millwright acted with impunity. Every test I had refused, he performed. Every sample I had denied him, he took. I thought I would die in that cell, if not from the torture, then because I would cease to interest him as a living test subject, and he would decide to study a drow's cadaver."

Ellis' ears rang. The knowledge jangled in her head until it nauseated her. Her father sat stiff as a board and stared past her at a small group of glowing lion's-ear mushrooms.

"Then your mother came to visit me."

Ellis held her breath. Surely, this meant Claire had come to the rescue.

"She apologized. She told me Millwright had threatened her with exposure to the media if she refused to help him. I gather she had committed significant ethical violations that would have created a scandal in the medical research community."

A death's-head smile stretched his lips. "His threat was not credible. Millwright would have destroyed his career along with hers, and he would not crush himself in a cave-in to spite his companion. Your mother is an extremely intelligent woman, so she knew that."

His face went back to neutral. Back to numb. "She chose to believe him because she, too, wished to continue the research. A person who kindly tends the rats is not so different than one who does so cruelly. By rejecting her, I had angered her, and thus, I became a deserving target for her studies."

Ellis wanted to cover her ears to keep from hearing more, but her father's words wriggled into her mind like a parasite. She would not have believed him, except...

Except that the DRI had served her pellets and water in rubber bowls and told her not to talk. They had not held her prisoner. They had claimed she was a *subject*.

Her father was telling the truth.

He sighed. "I thought you would lose respect for me if I told you how easily I had allowed myself to be sucked into betraying the drow."

She tried to speak, but her throat was dry. She sipped the cold tea. "I understand why you didn't tell me. How did you escape?"

Connor did not reply for a long time. "I convinced her we were in love again," he finally admitted, "and if she freed me, we could run away together."

"But you didn't."

"No. I ran away by myself. Back to my... What did you

call it? My hidey-hole." He closed his eyes in embarrassment.

Ellis touched his hand. She would choke on her guilt. "I shouldn't have said that."

He shrugged a shoulder. "Why not? You were right. Fear *has* kept me underground and made me advocate for total separation from humans. But as I have recently learned, ignorance can be as dangerous as knowledge."

"Did you know she was pregnant?" Ellis was not sure she wanted to know the answer.

Connor exhaled harshly. "No, I didn't. Your appearance was the best surprise of my life."

"Even though it ruined your relationship with Ilva?"

A rueful smile painted his face, and he met her gaze for what felt like the first time in hours. "I have made many mistakes in my life, Ellis Burton, but you are not one."

Ellis murmured, "This is very different from what Rose told me."

Connor's eyes warmed. "I'm glad you met her. Rose and her friends saw the best of your mother."

"They told me you went to see them after she disappeared. After I was born."

"You were *constantly* asking questions about your mother and the human world. I wondered if it was safe to visit. I believed that returning you to the homestead was your mother's way of expressing her love for you, and I still believe that. She understands that she is involved with people who do not have your best interests at heart.

"So, yes, I briefly returned to Los Angeles. My magic was powerful enough for me to remain invisible for a while, even during the day."

"How did you find her?"

He laughed softly. "I staked out her favorite burrito truck. She used to eat there several times a week, and I was sure that if she was still in the city, I would find her there. Miraculously, it was still operating.

"She arrived for lunch on day three, and I followed her to an office complex that was nondescript except for light-silk curtains. I waited, and when she left, Millwright was with her. They were friendly with each other, so I realized your mother was a lost cause.

"I was furious with her on your behalf. It would not be safe to visit if she was still working for the DRI. Millwright would have had no compunction about turning you into a test subject.

"I kept following her, and she went to see Rose and the others. She brought them a mushroom powder she should not have had."

"Could she have spored the mushroom samples you brought her?" Ellis wondered.

"Certainly, except she brought hyphellas."

"Those can't be grown outside caverns." Ellis knew that from personal experience. Hyphellas were among the most useful medicinal mushrooms the drow grew, so Ellis had tried to cultivate them in her shoe closet. It had resulted in a wall of mold.

Connor nodded. "Another drow had to have brought them to her. A few rangers had gone missing. I assumed Claire was involved in their disappearances."

"How?"

"She and Millwright had worked their way into the Defense Department's good graces and officially formed the DRI. The American military has so much funding that it is easy to siphon some off for morally questionable projects. They didn't have to steal supplies anymore. Stealing *people* would have been easy."

Ellis remembered the circle on Claire's map and bit her lip. "How did she know where to find you when she brought me back?"

Connor half-shrugged. "I knew she was eager to enter the caverns, so I promised I would show her the homestead if she freed me. I hoped her excitement would make her incautious and I could disappear. Unfortunately, I was still too weak from the lightsilk and had to run away. She must have followed me to the entrance. I'm not sure how she did that in the dark, but it's all I can think of."

Ellis imagined her father's desperate flight through the woods, with Claire stumbling behind him in pursuit. She would have been pregnant at the time.

"She was probably tracking you electronically and lost the signal when you went underground." That circumstance was painfully familiar.

"Perhaps."

Ellis frowned. "Wait. If she knew where an entrance was, why didn't she tell the DRI? They could have used drilling equipment or ground-penetrating radar, but I don't think they know any more now than they did then."

Connor pinched the bridge of his nose. "I cannot explain it."

Ellis blinked. "She cared about you. Dad, I think she loved you."

Anger sparked in her father's eyes. "You are eager to

think well of your flesh and blood. I understand, but you must not let your guard down around her."

Ellis did not comment. The conversation had sapped her remaining energy.

Connor saw the look on her face, softened, and touched her hand. "I will admit, I do not think she wants you to be harmed."

Ellis pushed his hand away. "Is that all?"

"There is one more thing." Her father drew a deep breath. "I wish to ask your forgiveness for keeping the truth from you for so long. It was a mistake."

The truth. Was that what her father had given her? Ellis shuddered. "I have to go."

"Let me finish tending those lightsilk burns. I know how they linger."

Ellis shook her head and stood. She could not look at his sorrowful face any longer.

"The homestead is in chaos," he protested. "You should take an escort."

She ignored him and left.

CHAPTER FOURTEEN

Ellis would rather be ripped apart by an angry mob than accept that she was not welcome in her home. Several of the drow she passed shot angry looks at her but kept their distance. How had she lived here without a single friend?

She desperately missed her shadow magic. It was the only thing that had granted her legitimacy in drow society.

The guards blocking the tunnel where Claire was being held raised their daggers at Ellis' approach. Behind them, two archers nocked arrows.

Ellis crossed her arms. "Let me through. I need to talk to my mother."

The guard on the left shook his head. He was one of her father's protégés—Jorel, if Ellis recalled. The young woman behind him was Mirelle. "No entrance. No exceptions."

Ellis glowered. "Your prisoner needs someone to tend her ankle. She already has trouble walking long distances. If you leave shattered bones untreated..."

"She is a captive. She does not need to walk long distances."

Jorel's calm sensibility made Ellis snap, and she rushed him.

She was lucky he did not run her through. Later, she wondered whether she had subconsciously wanted him to do so. Instead, he sheathed his dagger, blocked her kick, and dodged her punch.

Mirelle drew and fired in one smooth movement. Her aim was imperfect, and the arrow scored Ellis' upper arm and hit the wall.

"*Stop!*" The new voice was so authoritative that Ellis froze. For a second, she thought it was Claire, but Trissa emerged from the tunnel behind Mirelle and Jorel, medical bag in hand.

"She was trying to get through," Jorel protested.

Trissa met Ellis' gaze evenly. "Your mother is unconscious and will be for several hours. She needs rest more than she needs you hovering."

Ellis blushed. "Oh."

Trissa noticed the wound on Ellis' arm. "Are you in pain?"

Ellis shook her head, then shot a withering look at Mirelle. "Aim for the center of mass next time."

Mirelle flinched. "I didn't want to kill you. Your father…"

"Would tell you the same thing," Ellis interrupted, although she was not sure it was true.

"Come to my workroom," Trissa suggested and took Ellis by the arm. "I can look at that arrow…well, 'wound' seems like an overstatement."

Ellis let Trissa lead her away while Mirelle stared at her boots.

They stopped outside the infirmary. "Stay here," Trissa told her. "I have patients who were injured in the Great Hall, and I doubt your presence would calm them."

She meant, "Don't cause another ruckus," and Ellis could respect that. She leaned on the wall and tried not to think about what her father had told her. Allowing herself to spiral would end poorly. She decided to worry about saving Landon instead.

Trissa emerged carrying several small bags. "Let's go."

The passage led to a room with polished walls, and the tiled path split and curved around a pit of glowing orange crystals. Ellis basked in their warm light. She had become accustomed to sunlight and missed it.

Trissa nodded at the medallion keeper, who was busy with his rake at the far end of the room. He was alone. "Hello, Gondril. How's your mother's cough?"

He cheerfully returned her greeting, ignoring Ellis. "Much better, thank you."

Gondril dug through the crystals with his rake, which glowed at the metal's touch. He snagged a gold chain on one tine and flung it to Trissa. When she caught it, he nodded and smiled warmly. "Bring it back."

"Always."

Ellis was shocked. Access to the medallions was tightly controlled, so Landon had stolen them. Trissa had just waltzed in and asked.

Ellis followed Trissa to a tall arch hung with silk woven in geometric purples and blues in the residential area of the homestead. When Trissa swept the curtain aside, Ellis recognized much of the décor: a small lapis lazuli cup on a shelf near the bed nook, a well-polished dagger mounted above the double bed, and a stone table piled with scrolls and writing paper.

She frowned. "Why are we breaking into Landon's room? I didn't realize he'd moved."

Trissa's answering smile was pained. "This isn't Landon's room. It's *our* room."

"You *moved in* together?"

Landon had always been unsettled, jumping between jobs and romances. Sneaking out to concerts in LA with someone else was not something one did lightly. Ellis had known, on some level, that their relationship was serious.

She saw personal items unlikely to be Landon's, including a fringed silk robe. Ellis also saw Trissa's exhaustion, over which the healer pasted a brave smile.

"I know you've been through an ordeal, so I'm sorry to ask, but did you see him, Ellis? Is he still alive?"

Ellis perched on the bed beside Trissa. "I'm so sorry, Trissa. I didn't see him."

Trissa swallowed and nodded.

Ellis silently sighed. The DRI was awful, but they *had* put a tremendous effort into keeping her alive in captivity. They had fed her, and they had kept her "safe." Given what her father had told her about the DRI, it made sense that they would want to keep their test subjects alive.

"I can't be sure, but I think he's alive," Ellis told her. "He's valuable to them."

Trissa just folded her hands in her lap and nodded wordlessly.

"I'll save him, Trissa. I promise."

Trissa squeezed Ellis' hand. "You won't do it alone." She

pulled stoppered bottles and silk pouches of herbs out of her bags and arranged them on the blanket.

"Do you have more of the shadow magic potion?" Ellis asked.

"How much do you have left?"

"Um…"

Trissa looked up in alarm. "Tell me you didn't lose it."

"No! Well, I lost track of it for a few minutes, but…"

"You got it back?"

"Yes."

Trissa narrowed her eyes. "Spill."

"I, um, drank it."

Trissa went almost as pale as Ellis. "*What? There was enough potion in that bottle for *months*. What do you mean, you drank it?"

Ellis' cheeks heated up. "Kind of self-explanatory. I poured it into my mouth, and I swallowed it."

"*All* of it?" Trissa scooted away from Ellis as though she might explode if jostled.

Ellis smiled sheepishly. "The circumstances were desperate."

Trissa stared at Ellis for several seconds, then shook her head. "Did it work?"

Ellis barked a laugh. "Oh, it *worked*, all right. I figured out *really* fast why you told me to sip it. I dissolved a *significant* section of forest."

Trissa's eyes lit up with scientific curiosity. "*How* significant?"

Ellis recounted what had happened in Topanga Canyon and how she had used the potion to escape from the DRI.

When she finished, Trissa frowned, and Ellis' stomach swooped.

"What? Am I going to die? Sprout a third arm? Explode?"

"No. The effects should be minimal by this point, but I was hoping to use what you hadn't consumed to make more."

Ellis tilted her head. "You don't have the ingredients?"

Trissa pointed at a fist-sized cluster of growth medium tucked into an alcove beside the bed. Ellis had to lean over and squint to see the fungi emerging from the medium.

"I've been breeding a special varietal. I used the first crop for your batch, and the second..." Her voice trailed off, and she grimaced.

"What happened?"

"They were in the tunnel the guards caved in behind you," Trissa explained. "I didn't think anyone would mind if I took over some minor caverns for cultivation."

Ellis winced as she remembered the alcove full of chartreuse mushrooms. No wonder Ellis had not been able to remember their name. She had never seen them before.

Claire *had!* Ellis grumbled inventive invective, both human *and* drow.

"I know how you feel," Trissa dryly agreed.

"Why didn't you use a plot in the main cave? My test rack must be unoccupied."

Trissa shook her head. "I've kept it under wraps. Your father might have figured out what I was brewing, and if he had, he would have wanted to know who I was brewing it for. Then he would have wanted to know why you needed a potion that would restore your shadow magic."

She smiled. "I didn't want that kind of interference, and I didn't think you did, either."

Ellis sighed. "You're right about that." Given recent revelations, it might have served them all better to be more open with each other.

Trissa motioned at the tiny patch of mushrooms. "If the potion works, I don't want to use the only specimens in existence for a single batch."

"I'll do the best I can without it. Besides, you made a good point. The DRI is prepared to counter shadow magic. I shouldn't count on it anyway."

Trissa raised an eyebrow. "You keep saying, 'I.'"

"Those people are evil. You don't know what we're up against."

"Then you had better tell me. I have shadow magic in spades."

"I can't let you take that risk."

Trissa looked at Ellis as though she were throwing a tantrum. "Don't be ridiculous. I am coming to help Landon, and the longer we spend on this futile argument, the less time we'll have to develop an effective plan."

Ellis did not trust easily. She was so accustomed to lacking allies in the homestead that the prospect of support felt alien, but Trissa's jaw was set. If Ellis wanted to do this alone, she would have to sneak out, and given the current security situation and her lack of shadow magic, that would be difficult.

"Fine." She grabbed a quill and a sheet of paper. "Here's what I know about the DRI."

The drow made their quills from spider legs, so she decided to start there. Ellis dipped the quill in the ink and sketched what she remembered about the facility's layout while explaining the situation with the cave spiders.

Trissa was horrified. "They *trained* cave spiders? Who trains *cave spiders?*"

"Someone with a bunch of disposable goons."

Trissa picked up the finished diagram and meditatively waved it to dry the ink. When the ink no longer gleamed, she replaced it on the bed.

Ellis tapped the door that led to the sub-basement of the Bromeliad. "I doubt we'll make it down the stairs again. They'll have changed the locks on the elevator."

For the first time since she had been kidnapped, Ellis thought about Hector. She hoped he had not gotten in too much trouble. Amelia was a pragmatist, and with Ellis gone, someone had to run her mushroom grow-op. Hector was likely fine.

"Do you think you can find the exit your mother brought you out of?" Trissa asked.

Ellis nodded. She had been dazed and exhausted, but she was unlikely to forget information that could lead to her brother.

"Then that's our best bet," Trissa stated.

Ellis hesitated. The clicking of legs on concrete and metal echoed in her head. "I don't have an anti-spider beacon."

"Where are the other entrances?"

Ellis studied the diagram. Her memories of leaving the facility were clear, thanks to her photographic memory, but the halls had looked so similar that it was hard to know what direction she had been going.

She crossed one off. They had made three lefts, not four

when they'd left the holding cells. Ellis shivered at the memory of the electrified floor, then shook her head. She did not have enough information.

The DRI facility was extensive. Maybe they could dig down from the basement of a building near the park. "How's your tunneling?"

"I can feed someone magic, but I'm garbage at big rock-work. I was made for small scale. Veins, arteries—that kind of thing."

"Those are the tunnels of the body," Ellis ventured, but Trissa shook her head. That was disappointing. A tunnel was their best shot. Without one, Ellis did not think they could escape the extra guards posted at the homestead's entrances.

Trissa read Ellis' mind. "I thought we could leave through the *second* most abandoned exit, seeing as the first one was caved in."

Ellis tried not to take the jab to heart. "That might be too obvious. Third?"

Trissa laughed. "Reasonable."

Ellis tapped the quill too hard, and the tip broke off. An inky stain spread across a corridor. She folded the paper in half to blot it, then crumpled it and flung it to the floor. "We need more information, but we'll have to make do. We should leave when the council session starts. My father's and Ilva's proposals will keep them busy for hours."

"Agreed. In the meantime, we should rest."

"I want to take a bath." Ellis' mouth watered at the thought of a plunge in the homestead's hot springs since she was covered in grime. Washing it off might help with her lingering distress.

"I can bring you a basin of water." Trissa offered.

Ellis scowled. She did not want a sponge bath. She wanted to soak. The thought of plunging into the hot water pulled her toward the silk curtain. As she was about to fling it aside, Trissa blocked her. "Ellis, you can't."

Ellis glared. She could smell the sulfur and feel the smooth stone on the soles of her feet. "Just because I'm walking into certain death doesn't mean I have to smell like it."

Trissa slapped her.

Ellis had been hit harder. Hell, Ellis had been hit harder by humans. She was more surprised than hurt. "Ow! Calm down. It's just a *bath*! Mother Beneath."

"We are *not* walking into certain death."

Ellis' eyebrows drew together in confusion. "I told you that you didn't have to come. If you're having second thoughts, I'll do it myself."

Trissa crossed her arms. "I'm not having second thoughts. I understand that we're taking a risk, but if you're only going because you hope the DRI will shoot you, I can't let you. If it were truly hopeless, Landon wouldn't want you killed, and he wouldn't want you to drum up trouble beforehand."

Ellis blinked. "What?"

Trissa held back an eye-roll with a supreme effort of will. "You can't wander around the homestead with things as tense as they are now. Someone at the baths could make you slip or dissolve your head with shadow magic and claim self-defense. Or worse."

"What would be worse than *dissolving my head*?" Ellis asked incredulously.

Trissa spoke over her, her words a-tumble. "If you died, I'd have to rescue Landon on my own, and I want him to have the best shot, so I need you not to be an idiot!"

"I can take care of myself," Ellis lied. In truth, she felt brittle. What she had learned had rattled and weakened her, and she felt close to snapping under the weight of the looming task. Hence the desire for a fucking *bath*.

Trissa did not back down. "This isn't about taking care of yourself. You've made your independence *quite* clear. No, Ellis, it's about taking care of *me* so I can infiltrate the DRI and save Landon. *That's* what we're walking into. A rescue mission, *not* certain death."

"*Un*certain death?" Ellis ventured.

"I'll accept uncertain death. Hopelessness is a slippery slope, Ellis."

"I still want to take a bath," Ellis complained.

Trissa's eyes narrowed to black slits. "You don't want a bath. You want a fight."

Ellis sighed. Trissa was right. Working out her troubles via boot-to-face connections always made her feel better.

She churlishly flung herself on the bed. "Fine! You're the one who has to smell me."

Trissa did not comment, just bustled around the room. Ellis tuned her out until a cool hand touched her shoulder. Ellis opened her eyes and found Trissa offering her Landon's lapis lazuli cup.

"Drink this. It'll help you rest."

If she could not relax in a deep pool, a deep sleep would have to do. Ellis settled into Trissa's and Landon's pillows and drank. The tea tasted like rocks and earth, and it pulled her into comforting darkness.

CHAPTER FIFTEEN

When Ellis woke up, two stuffed silk packs waited on the sideboard. Trissa was finishing her half of a light breakfast of mushroom tea and salted fish. A small brazier in the corner was lit, and a clay pot of water bubbled atop it, wafting sulfuric fumes.

"I brought you a bath," Trissa informed her.

Ellis blushed. "You didn't have to do that."

Trissa's nose wrinkled. "I changed my mind while you were asleep. You were right. I *do* have to smell you."

Ellis chuckled. "Thanks."

"Thank me by being ready when I return." She drained her tea and hurried away.

The scrub-down was not the enveloping plunge about which she had fantasized, but it was hot. Ellis felt much better after washing away the dirt. She dried herself with the towel Trissa had left beside the brazier, then inspected the crystal-silk jumpsuit laid out on the bed. It was of high enough quality that it would stop at least one bullet.

She dressed, then strapped Landon's dagger to her

waist. The blade had been a gift from their grandfather. He might not have approved of Ellis taking it, but she did not think Landon would mind. If he did, they would have plenty of time to fight about it later.

True to her word, when Trissa returned, Ellis was waiting with her pack belted tight across her chest. Unfortunately, the circles under Trissa's eyes had deepened.

Ellis frowned. "Is everything all right?"

Trissa curled her fingers around her pack's straps and avoided Ellis' gaze. "I went to check on your mother before we left to see if her ankle bones were knitting properly. I'm not the only competent healer in the homestead—Florian's better at bones—but I'm not sure anyone else would… consider her care important."

Ellis appreciated that, but Trissa was being cagey. "Has her injury worsened?"

The infirmarians had mushrooms for infections and pain. Simple medical complications did not explain the level of distress on Trissa's face.

"She's gone."

The words thudded dully in Ellis' ears. "*What?*"

"She's missing," Trissa hastily clarified. "And with her injured ankle…"

Ellis was breathless with panic. "We can worry about her after we find her."

Either Claire had escaped, or someone had taken her… or she was dead. The thought hit Ellis like an anvil.

Then again, it was difficult to obliterate someone with shadow magic without leaving any trace. Most mages could not target a spell that precisely and left collateral damage or…pieces. Plus, anyone who dared attack Claire would have faced Connor's wrath. She had been under his protection.

Unless Connor had killed her.

Ellis refused to consider the possibility. "How long has she been gone?"

"I don't know."

"What did the guards say?"

"They didn't see anything."

They had probably been involved. Ellis scowled, strode out of the room, and headed for the cells, ignoring Trissa's shouts.

She skirted the mushroom tunnels to avoid the Great Hall. As she passed an alcove, a hand wrapped around her wrist and pulled her in.

Ellis yelped and reached for her dagger, but the person blocked her. A moment later, a shadow magic shroud dissolved to reveal her father.

"*Fuck!*" Ellis whispered. Her father pursed his lips, and she rolled her eyes. "If you don't want me to curse, don't startle me. Where's Mom?"

His eyes flashed, and it took Ellis a second to realize that he was angry she had called Claire "Mom." *Whatever.*

"Have you checked the cells? Is she dead?" Ellis demanded.

"No."

Footsteps in the corridor prompted Connor to prepare another shroud, but he relaxed when Trissa appeared, breathing hard.

The infirmarian frowned when she saw Connor with Ellis. "Uh, hi."

Connor ignored the greeting and gestured in the direction from which they had appeared. "Come with me," he ordered.

Ellis glared. "I am not going *anywhere* until you tell me where Claire is."

Connor's frown turned into a scowl. After a pause, he motioned with his right hand, and a figure appeared in the shadows. Her pale skin glowed in the dim light from the hall. Her shoulders were hunched, and she rested her weight on one foot, but the silhouette was unmistakable. It was Claire.

Ellis blinked. "What the *hell?*"

Connor was unperturbed. "If we don't reach the Trunks soon, we'll miss our window."

"Our window for *what?*"

Ellis growled in exasperation. She was speaking to Connor's back. He was jogging down the hall toward the Trunks.

The Trunks was a cluster of vertical tunnels that opened into the Angeles National Forest. The rangers used them to collect lumber and herbs from the surface and keep an eye on the exterior of the homestead.

One was standing guard at the entrance. Connor had shrouded them with help from Trissa, so Ellis expected them to sneak past. However, Connor whistled a rhythmic melody, and the guard plastered himself to the side of the tunnel and began mouthing numbers, counting down from thirty.

That had to be what Connor had meant by "our window." Ellis' father was calling in favors, but Ellis did not understand why. Nothing he had told Ellis suggested he harbored sufficient warmth for Claire to rescue her. Quite the opposite.

When they emerged from the Trunks into the night, Ellis put her hands on her hips and planted her feet. "What is going *on?*"

Claire exited behind her and leaned against a tree. Trissa had bound Claire's ankle and treated her, but her mother was pale and breathed hard from the climb.

Connor noticed that and handed Claire a bottle of rustcap juice. Their fingers brushed when she took it, and disgust crossed his face. Ellis was glad that Claire was too unwell to notice as she gratefully gulped the dark liquid.

"You were leaving to save Landon," Connor stated.

Ellis and Trissa traded glances. Denying it was pointless.

"Yeah, that was the plan," Ellis admitted. "But why is Claire here? I thought you didn't trust her."

Connor's lips tightened. "I don't, but she has information we need."

Ellis pinned her mother with a stare. "Even though 'you haven't worked there in years?'"

Claire winced but did not protest.

Ellis scoffed. "What if she lies to us? Or betrays us?"

Connor tilted his head, confused. "She's not an *ally.* She's a *hostage.*"

That surprised Claire and Ellis. "Oh," Ellis muttered, and Claire echoed her.

Connor whistled another pattern, and Ellis stiffened as several drow appeared out of the darkness: Rollo, who had caved the tunnel in behind her, Jorel, who had turned her away from the cells, and Mirelle, the archer who had failed to shoot her.

Ellis raised an eyebrow. "I hope your aim is better next time."

Mirelle snorted.

Ellis recognized Welton, Ulivi, and Frella, but there were others whose faces she could not place. Connor had assembled a ragtag force a dozen strong. They were all young, but they bristled with weaponry and determination, and all looked at Connor with awe. *You might feel differently if he was your dad.*

Something crashed through the undergrowth, and the little militia sprang into action, nocking arrows and unsheathing daggers. Ellis could tell it was an animal, not a human. Maybe a bear?

Ellis gasped as the shape came around a boulder into the moonlight. *"Flower!"*

Mirelle drew her bow and aimed at the pit bull's heart. Ellis regretted her earlier advice.

"Put your weapons down! Please!"

The drow hesitated long enough for Flower to stop in front of Ellis and excitedly wag her tail.

Tears welled in Ellis' eyes, and her throat felt thick. "You waited."

Flower woofed. Ellis did not need Percy to translate. *Of course.*

Ellis knelt and fished in her pocket. "You should have gone somewhere safe," she admonished. Flower nuzzled her hand in thanks for the proffered jerky.

The drow exchanged wary glances, but no one objected.

They relaxed when Connor approached and patted Flower's head. The pit bull wagged her silver tail harder.

Without further ado, Connor led them into the forest, and Ellis' confidence surged. They would not need to find another entrance. With this many drow, they could tunnel.

CHAPTER SIXTEEN

As they traveled, Connor drifted between clusters of drow. Whenever he left Claire's side, another drow kept an eye on her, although she posed little threat without weapons or lightsilk.

Nonetheless, Ellis kept her distance. She was not concerned about her safety. Not only did her mother have no weapons, but she was injured. However, Ellis could not afford to lose focus, and looking at her mother made her jittery and upset.

Connor rejoined Ellis when they heard traffic in the distance. "Your grandmother's tactics manuals included tricks for traveling in groups in the human world. The surface has become brighter and louder since her heyday, but the principles are still sound."

Ellis wished she had asked Nan Elandra more about her adventures in the human world. She had been alive in the Roaring Twenties and might have seen old Hollywood.

"You should let me lead this mission," Ellis told him.

Connor opened his mouth to reply, but she cut him off.

"I have the most recent fighting experience against humans, including the DRI, and I'm the only one who's been in that facility."

"The only *drow*, yes." Connor glanced at Claire.

"I might have the easiest time getting information from her." The thought made her feel dirty, but she could not afford to keep her hands clean any longer.

Connor clicked his tongue. "I'm not sure that's true. I believe she subconsciously knows the DRI is unethical, and she wishes to reveal her dark side to you the least."

"We'll have to chance it. I don't see any other way."

Her father considered her words for several seconds, then nodded. "Then you may lead this mission. You've proven to be a ferocious fighter."

Ellis swelled with pride, but he tempered his words with caution. "However, your anger toward me and her must wait. There will be time for a reckoning later. Right now, we need information. Slugs cluster on sugarcaps."

It was the drow's way of saying, "You catch more flies with honey than vinegar." Ellis had never understood why you would want to catch flies *or* slugs. Regardless, her father was right. "We'll put our differences aside until Landon's safe."

Connor nodded again, then proceeded down the line, leaving Ellis a few paces behind Claire. Ellis drew a deep breath and decided there was no time like the present.

She walked up beside her mother. "How's your ankle?"

Claire was struggling despite the slow pace. She hissed as she stepped on a rock that shifted. "It hurts, but not as much as it did a few hours ago. While I can't say I enjoyed feeling my bones grow—there's something to be said for plaster casts—it's amazing that I can walk.

"What was in that medicine? It tasted like hot compost water, but it healed my shattered ankle in half an hour. I tried to pour the second dose onto a cloth, but she saw me. Do you have more?"

Ellis clenched her teeth. Her mother's desire to obtain a mushroom sample grated on her nerves, but she reminded herself of the slugs and the flies. "Are you in pain?"

Claire shrugged. "Yes, but there's nothing for it. The bones have healed as much as they can without time and rest. I want a sample to study back at my lab."

Ellis made a noise in the back of her throat at the mention of the lab.

"Are you all right?" her mother asked.

"'Your lab' is holding my brother like a caged rat. When we rescue him…"

Her voice trailed off. She wanted to say, "We'll dissolve the place from the inside out until it crumples like a can in a trash compactor," and maybe, "We'll hunt down everyone who worked there," but the flies and the slugs would not catch themselves.

She kept her tone light. "After we've rescued him, we'll talk more." Claire nodded and looked relieved, so Ellis continued. "On that note, I need to know more about the layout of the lab. I know about the entrance in the Bromeliad's basement and the emergency exit shaft in the park. Are there others?"

"There's an entrance under a military recruiting booth in a strip mall downtown."

Ellis grimaced. Having the military discover their sortie was the last thing they needed. "What else?"

Claire bit her lip. "Once upon a time, there was an entrance in a subway maintenance access shaft, but no one ever used it, so they bricked it up."

Ellis' body prickled with adrenaline. The drow could punch through a few feet of bricks and concrete in seconds. "How far is it from the prison cells?"

The word "prison" startled Claire. She hid it, but Ellis noticed. Evidently, Claire considered the cages to be something other than a prison.

"That entrance is across the facility from the...prison cells."

"What do *you* call them?" The question slipped out before Ellis could stop herself. Claire's posture became guarded, and Ellis forced herself to let it go. "Never mind. How many people are down there?"

"About a hundred at any time, half of whom are scientists who won't engage in an armed struggle."

Fifty people. Fifteen drow and one dog against fifty soldiers, give or take.

Ellis' evaluation of their odds must have been plain since Claire offered, "If we move quickly, that might not be a problem. Do you remember that news story at the diner about the senator visiting military facilities throughout the state? The DRI is on her itinerary."

Ellis' eyebrows rose. "When?"

"Thursday morning at ten o'clock."

Ellis realized she had lost track of what day it was. Trissa looked up from the screen of her phone. "That's six hours from now."

Ellis stared at the small, bright rectangle. "You have a *phone?*"

"Landon gave it to me."

Claire's gaze sparkled with interest. The cold curiosity made Ellis uneasy, but she set it aside and pressed on. "Will there be increased security because of the senator?"

Claire shrugged. "Some, but mostly around her. If *her* people realize something's wrong, you're toast, but I'd bet cold hard cash that Malcolm will do his damnedest to cover up anything that happens during her visit. He'll send a small team to address any disturbance and pretend that nothing's happening. No alarms. No chaos."

"Are you sure about that? What if he calls in the SEALs at the first sign of trouble?"

"He won't."

"How can you be sure?"

"I've known him for a long time. He won't risk appearing imperfect."

Ellis gnawed on her lip. "In that case, we need to move faster. Pick up the pace, everyone."

Claire tripped on a root, stumbled, and winced. Ellis did not care. She would carry Claire if she had to to save her brother.

CHAPTER SEVENTEEN

Charlie and Liza passed two lab-coated researchers who were arguing loudly. One woman's eyelid was twitching. "Why is everyone so tense?" he whispered to his partner.

"There's a rumor that Senator Chan wants to shut the DRI down," Liza replied. "It's top secret, so hardly anyone knows what it does. Thus, it's easy to propose cutting it."

Charlie saw more cracks in the DRI's pristine veneer with every passing moment. For one, none of the security cameras were operational, which explained why Morrissey had escaped so easily. His next clue had been his mismatched uniform. The lightsilk overshirt barely fit. Every time he moved, he thought the sleeves would rip.

Morrissey had not wanted to wear it. He remembered Ellis' scream when the fabric touched her skin. In the end, he had put it on rather than draw attention to himself.

"Has anyone else tried to shut the DRI down?" he asked. Earlier, they had interrupted several researchers muttering about job searches.

Liza shrugged. "I heard a few people mention an NSA

visit a while back, but I guess Millwright convinced them to keep the place going. I get the sense that he's very… persuasive."

That was one word for it. Morrissey thought everyone in the DRI was *afraid* of their boss. Millwright struck him as someone who confused domination with leadership. Suddenly, he missed Jericho.

Liza nudged him. "Snap out of it."

Morrissey straightened. She could always tell when his mind wandered. "Where to, boss?"

Liza pulled a small plastic object from her pocket and grimaced. "We're on feeding duty." The object had a button. When she pressed it, the lights overhead flashed, and a low tone emanated from speakers placed at intervals along the walls.

Feeding Great Dane-sized spiders was a dangerous job, but it was not complicated. It consisted of dumping dog food into a concrete room while ignoring the flashing lights and alarms that kept the spiders in the vents where you could not see them.

Morrissey heaved a sigh of relief when they were finished. No sooner had the door latched behind them than Liza's phone beeped with a message.

"Look sharp. The senator's here."

CHAPTER EIGHTEEN

There had been one tense moment in the subway tunnels. The headlights of a train had borne down on them in a section of tunnel in which it was clear that plastering themselves against the concrete walls would not suffice.

Connor had been forced to create a shallow alcove in the rock, and they huddled in it while the train passed. Ellis wondered what the maintenance staff would think when they discovered it.

Otherwise, the militia had made good time. They stood outside the bricked-up entrance to the DRI while Ellis gave her final directives.

"Our primary mission is to rescue Landon," she told them. "They'll know we're here as soon as we break through, and they have lightsilk nets and confetti guns." Seeing the confused expressions on some of the drow's faces, she hastily explained the weaponry.

"That's why you have to work in teams," she finished. "The lightsilk burns like hell, and if you take enough damage from it, you might lose access to your shadow magic. Look after each other and take up the slack for anyone who's incapacitated."

Several drow turned green, but everyone nodded.

Ellis went on. "Fortunately, our entry point is near the armory. We'll secure that first, then go for the prison cells. Don't kill anyone you don't have to, but don't hesitate if you do. Remember, the DRI doesn't consider drow to be people. They will kill you like we crush a bug underfoot."

Ellis leveled a hard look at her mother. Claire would not meet her gaze, and her expression was frozen and unreadable.

Focus on Landon. Ellis drew a deep breath. "Conserve your energy to maintain invisibility. It's tempting to blast holes in this place, but doing so will alert them to our location. Questions?"

She answered a few inquiries about the DRI's lightsilk defenses, then put the tunneling team to work. Connor led the group in dissolving the bricks layer by layer.

Ellis approached Claire, who was observing the display of magic. "It's miraculous," she murmured.

Ellis ignored her. "Mom." When Claire looked at her, Ellis screwed up her courage. "If you lie to me, deceive us in any way, or try to thwart this mission, I will never speak to you again. If I can help it, you will never see my face."

"Oh, Ellis." Claire took her daughter's hand. Out of the corner of her eye, Ellis saw Connor glance over uneasily. "I've only ever wanted to help people. If you understood more—"

Ellis yanked her hand away. "Stop. I don't want to talk about this. I only want you to acknowledge that you heard me."

"I'm here to help you," Claire protested.

Ellis crossed her arms and waited.

Finally, Claire sighed. " I heard you. Everything I've said about this facility is true."

"Thank you."

Ellis returned to her father. The tunnel was now four feet deep. A young woman named Frella, whose skin was an unusual pale blue, was on the floor, peering through a tiny guide hole.

Frella stood and brushed the dust from her clothes. "About a hand's breadth remaining."

Ellis nodded, then looked down as a soft *woof* came from the vicinity of her feet. Flower sat patiently beside Ellis and watched the tunnel deepen.

Ellis scratched Flower's head. "You can't come with us, girl."

One of Flower's ears rose, and she looked at Ellis witheringly.

"You have to wait here while we're inside," Ellis insisted.

Flower huffed and pointedly ignored Ellis' continued scratches.

Ellis sighed. Even if Flower had a collar, Ellis had no leash, and anything she jerry-rigged was unlikely to constrain the powerfully built dog.

"Fine. You can come, but stay glued to my side. You understand?"

A satisfied *woof* was the only response.

Ellis approached Trissa. Claire would be in Connor's group. Ellis hoped she had made the right decision by pairing them and their history would motivate rather than distract them. She was certain he would not underestimate Claire.

Her father flattened his palms and gently pushed, and what was left of the wall disappeared.

Ellis' heart rate spiked with adrenaline as first Connor's group, then the other disappeared as well. Trissa, Jorel, and Mirelle wrapped Ellis' cluster in shadow magic, and the drow poured through the tunnel into the DRI.

The blazing overhead lights were punishing. Ellis wondered if they could have shut off the electricity, but that would have given them away. On her left, Jorel's shoulders tensed as he struggled to maintain his magic under the fluorescents. He appeared to be getting the hang of it, although judging by the way Trissa's hands were moving, she was feeding him power. She gave him an encouraging smile, too. Ellis liked Trissa a lot.

Connor and Claire walked side by side ahead of her. Their shoulders touched, and the sight tugged at Ellis' heart. A forced march through an evil lab was not the happy family reunion she had imagined.

Claire led them to the armory's door, and Connor gestured Ellis forward. She pressed her ear to the white laminate. There were people inside.

"There are only two confetti canisters in that thing, so shoot like you mean it. The safesilk hurts, but it only removes their magical abilities. They can still walk over and punch you in the face."

"I don't want to carry this shit, Liza," a man replied.

It was Liza Laponte and Charlie Morrissey. Ellis' heart soared, then plummeted, and finally settled into a rapid, frantic ostinato. He *had* turned against her.

"If you'd seen the look on Ellis' face when it touched her! That shit is brutal."

Maybe he had not.

"So is getting your head sliced off. If you'd prefer to rain bullets into the void, be my guest. Safesilk is non-lethal and a lot kinder than anything the MECs will do if they escape."

Ellis held her breath as she waited for Charlie's response, but she only heard a metallic click, a rustle, and footsteps. She dove aside as the door swung open, and the other dark elves scrambled away with an agility that would have been amusing if Liza and Charlie had not been covered in lightsilk.

Ellis recognized the funnel shape of a confetti gun at Charlie's hip. His pragmatism had overridden his moral objections.

Liza paused to tie her shoe beside Mirelle, who had flattened herself against the wall. Jorel raised his bow. Ellis almost spoke, but Trissa shook her head, and Jorel's bow dropped. Liza stood, and she and Charlie walked on.

Trissa motioned for everyone to wait, then glanced up and down the corridor and slipped into the armory. Curious, Ellis followed. It was nearly ten o'clock, so they had little time to waste, but she trusted the woman's judgment.

Trissa hastily retrieved a pair of oiled metal tongs, a set of shears, and a silk bag from her medical kit. Then, she snipped off the corner of a lightsilk net rolled up on a metal shelf.

"Be careful," Ellis sharply whispered.

Trissa rolled her eyes and snared the scrap of fabric with her tongs. She peered at it, then stuffed it in the bag.

She tightly rolled the top, double-knotted it, and stuffed it into a second sack for good measure.

"What are you doing?" Ellis asked as they re-entered the corridor.

"Taking a sample. I want to know why their lightsilk is different from ours."

"Smart girl."

Ellis jumped. That was Claire's voice, emanating from elsewhere in the hall. A twinge of envy stabbed Ellis in the gut. She had not heard her mother use that tone of approval when speaking to *her*.

She quashed her grumpy subconscious and motioned down the corridor. They had to move. Trissa shook her head and did something complicated with her hands. Then Ellis could see Connor's group.

Her father's face was grim. "We need to bring down the armory."

Ellis cocked her head. *What happened to me being in charge?* "That will give away our position," she countered.

"Yes, but it will also seriously limit the DRI's ability to respond. We'll need to move fast afterward."

Trissa, Jorel, and Connor raised their hands. The first sign of anything occurring was a low whine from Flower, who was staring at the ceiling. A deep rumble heralded a crack in the corridor's ceiling as the adjacent room's ceiling collapsed.

The drow militia hurried down the tunnel as the first chips of plaster flaked off, invisible against the white laminate door. Next stop, Landon.

CHAPTER NINETEEN

Morrissey shivered as he and Liza left the armory. The DRI facility was cool—so many people wandered around in full body armor, he supposed they did not notice—but for whatever reason, this corridor felt colder than usual.

Liza's phone beeped after they turned the corner, and she pulled up short. "Millwright's called an all-hands meeting in the zoo."

"What's the zoo?"

She paused for a long time before responding. "It's where they keep the MECs."

He gaped at her. "You call it 'the zoo?'"

Liza turned before he could see her face. "Technically, it's Hall A, but no one will know what you're talking about if you call it that. Let's go."

Reluctantly, he followed. A minute later, a rumble echoed down the hall, and the soles of Morrissey's boots vibrated. "What was that?"

Liza shrugged. "Minor quake. Don't worry about it.

This place is so far down that we feel them, but it's built on giant springs like NORAD."

The rumbling did not stop, but Liza dragged Charlie away. "Maybe the meeting's about architectural problems," she ventured. She did not sound convinced.

Despite its name, the zoo was underwhelming. It was impressively large, though he did not want to think about the engineering involved in creating a cavern under Los Angeles the size of a football field. He had expected noise and chaos like the animal lab. Instead, its rows of field tents were eerily quiet. Maybe no MECs were inside.

He and Liza joined a group about eighty strong at the edge of the room. Millwright stood beside a microphone attached to a small amplifier, still wearing the ridiculous paisley lab coat and bowtie.

Senator Chan was beside him. She was elegantly dressed in a dark suit. If she had an opinion about Millwright's fashion choices, they did not show on her face. She dwarfed Millwright, and her sleek dark hair was shot through with strands of white. She was accompanied by a military attaché in a dress uniform. Beside her, Millwright bore a faint resemblance to a clown.

"Does he always dress like that?" Morrissey murmured.

"This is downright subdued for him," Liza replied under her breath.

Two nearby soldiers chuckled. Liza introduced Charlie, but the ice-breakers were interrupted by Millwright tapping the microphone. Morrissey could barely see the short man over the crowd, but he could hear him.

Millwright made perfunctory opening remarks about how honored the DRI was to host Senator Chan. "The DRI is an open book, Senator. Whatever you'd like to see and whoever you'd like to speak to, your wish is my command."

The senator's responding smile was a carefully honed expression that showed off recently whitened teeth. "Thank you, Dr. Millwright. I look forward to learning more about your work. I'll be pulling many of you aside for individual conversations, but before that, it's time to let the dog see the rabbit."

The assembly shifted in time for Morrissey to see Millwright's eyes go cold. He forced the smile back to life before saying in a sing-song voice, "Certainly. Class dismissed!"

The drow progressed through the facility until they reached the cavernous hall in which Landon was being held. Ellis overheard two guards complaining about mandatory overtime inside the doors.

She raised her eyebrows at Trissa, motioned at the group, and put a finger to her lips.

Trissa nodded and gestured, then whispered, "We're silenced."

"We need a distraction," Ellis told them. "Any ideas?"

The drow discussed splitting up to draw the guards away, but Trissa was concerned that alerting the DRI to the presence of invisible intruders would result in chaos.

Flower bumped Ellis' knee, and she told the dog to sit. Flower obeyed but nudged Ellis' leg again.

"*What*, Flower?"

The dog raised a paw.

Ellis' jaw dropped. "Are you *volunteering?*"

Connor looked flabbergasted. Trissa tilted her head. Claire's eyes narrowed. "Are you sure she's not Millwright's?"

Flower's hackles rose, and Ellis shook her head. "Flower is her own dog."

Ellis considered it. A dog would raise questions, but not the kind that would lead to lightsilk confetti flooding the halls.

"Does the DRI use guard dogs?" she asked Claire.

"No, but—"

Ellis had no time for this. "But what?"

"Millwright does animal testing."

"On *dogs?*"

Claire's response was grim. "Among other animals."

Ellis' lips tightened to a thin line. "If they think Flower's an escaped experiment, they'll shoot her."

"I doubt that," Claire replied. "No one here wants to piss Millwright off, and killing one of his subjects would *infuriate* him. At worst, they'll tranquilize her."

Ellis hated the idea of someone knocking her loyal pup out, but it was the best option. She crouched and took Flower's head between her hands. "All right. Be careful. Look friendly. If anyone points a gun at you, *play dead.*"

Flower woofed.

"Let her out," Ellis told Trissa.

The drow removed the shroud over Flower, and the dog trotted to the end of the hall. Her nails clicked on the floor.

"Everyone out of the way," Ellis instructed. They plastered themselves against the walls and waited.

Flower went crazy.

Ellis had heard the dog bark, but Flower, who had gotten smarter the longer she lived with Percy, typically communicated in a sane fashion. Now, she lost her shit.

The people speaking in the other room paused, and one asked, "Do you hear that?" When Flower's tirade continued, a guard opened the door and peered down the corridor. "What the fuck? Jimmy, look at this."

A second man joined the first. "Oh, shit." He reached for his gun, but his friend stopped him. Ellis relaxed. Her mother had been right.

Satisfied that she had the guards' attention, Flower stopped barking. She wagged her tail and trotted toward the guards with her tongue lolling out, looking adorable. *Smart dog.*

The first guard smiled and beckoned. "Come here, pooch. Who's a good dog?"

Flower cheerfully barked, then trotted away.

The guard followed. "Go grab a dart gun," he told the other man.

"We can't leave our post."

The first man rolled his eyes. "Our best men are in the zoo, and they're all armed. I don't want feeding duty again. Those spiders creep me out."

The second guard heaved a long sigh, then followed his friend down the corridor.

It was now or never. Ellis slipped through the door.

There were plenty of people in the hall but no one in their immediate vicinity. Ellis prayed no one would look their way. At the moment, everyone was clustered around one tent.

The tents. Ellis got dizzy. The buzzing of the fluorescent lights became a drone, then a roar, and electricity crackled through her feet as someone yelled, *"MECs don't talk!"*

Ellis trembled. Rubber bowls. She had to stand on her rubber bowls to avoid the electricity, but she did not know where they were. The light was too bright and too loud.

"Ellis!"

The voice broke through her cocoon of fear. Strong hands grabbed her upper arms. They would put her in a tent. Why had she come back? She thrashed against her captor.

"Ellis!"

Her father's face swam into view, followed by Trissa's. Connor was holding her, and Trissa was leaning over his shoulder.

"You're okay, Ellis," Trissa assured her.

"Is she hurt?" Claire asked.

"Not physically," her father grimly replied.

The question struck Ellis as nonsensical. What other way could she be hurt?

Ellis stared at the ceiling of the cavern far above. The rough stone reminded her of the homestead, and her breathing slowed. She closed her eyes.

When she opened them, she was on the floor. Her father was still leaning over her with Trissa at his shoulder, but Ellis' mother was nowhere to be seen.

Ellis took Trissa's offered hand and got to her feet. She rubbed her temples.

Connor spotted Claire at the edge of the group of drow and shot over to her, one hand clawed to gather shadow magic. He grabbed Claire's shoulder, and she flinched. "You will *not* betray us," Connor hissed.

Claire did not shake off his hand. She pointed at the crowd around the tent. "I'm not going anywhere. The senator is there."

"You cannot blame me for my caution," Connor growled.

Claire cast a sorrowful look at Ellis, who was still shaking. She had glanced at the tent when her mother had pointed, and the soles of her feet prickled, but she stayed upright.

"I know," Claire murmured, then turned away.

Ellis approached with Trissa on her heels. "We can't cut through the lightsilk coverings on the cages. Not with shadow magic, anyway. I'll rip them down by hand."

"No. I'll do that," Claire firmly stated.

Connor nodded, then surveyed the tents. "Where is Landon?"

"I'm not sure," Claire admitted. "I don't come to the z—" She stopped herself. "I don't come down here often. When I rescued Ellis, there were four other MECs in the facility." *Four?* Who were the other three?

"Four other *drow*," Connor corrected. Claire did not argue.

"We have to rescue all of them," Ellis insisted.

Connor's face was grave, and Claire's was unreadable. Finally, the doctor hesitantly ventured, "The other MECs might not respond well to rescue."

Ellis narrowed her eyes. "What do you mean?"

"They've been held under…challenging conditions."

"You mean they've been tortured."

Claire shook her head so violently that Ellis thought it might fly off. "We're a research facility, not Guantanamo. We do *not* torture our subjects."

"Yet you call them 'subjects!'" Ellis' voice rose so sharply that Trissa looked around nervously to make sure the outburst had not pierced their envelope of shadow magic. "*Bullshit,* you don't torture people. The floors are *electrified.*"

"That's a training reinforcement tool." Claire spoke thoughtlessly, as though she had memorized the words in a foreign language. Ellis' vision blurred with a surge of disgust. Her mother *believed* what she was saying.

The other drow's expressions darkened, and Rollo's hand strayed to the hilt of his dagger. Connor gave him a warning look, and he crossed his arms instead.

Ellis spoke through gritted teeth. "If you're so comfortable with how you treat your subjects, why did you break me out?"

"That's different. You're...my daughter."

Ellis didn't doubt that Claire had intended to say, "You're human."

"I'm not only *your* daughter." Ellis stepped back to stand beside her father. They might not look alike, but she squared her shoulders and hoped her allegiance was clear.

Connor raised a hand to ease the tension. "We will rescue all the drow we can."

His people reluctantly nodded. Claire still looked uneasy, but it was nothing to how sick Ellis felt when she looked at her mother.

Connor waved them toward the DRI staff clustered around the senator. As they threaded between the tents, Claire grasped at Ellis' sleeve. "Ellis, you must understand that the research we're doing is valuable. It could save thousands of lives."

Ellis looked everywhere but at her mother's face. Her gaze landed on yet another tent. "That tent taught me everything I need to know about the value of your *research.*"

They were steps from the senator's group. Connor shushed them as they approached. A guard was about to pull back the lightsilk curtain. He was flanked by two others, one carrying a lightsilk confetti gun and the other an assault rifle.

"I thought Dr. Burton would be here to lead the tour," Senator Chan remarked.

Millwright's smile was artificially bright. "It *is* a shame she's out sick, but you're in good hands."

A nervous, thin-faced man in a white lab coat cleared his throat. "I'm Dr. Everly, Senator, taking over from Dr. Burton. Before you see the first MEC, I have to warn you. They appear similar to humans aside from being purple, but they more closely resemble primates such as orang-utans or gorillas. They don't have language, and they can be quite violent."

Ellis unsheathed her grandfather's dagger. He was right about one thing. She would show these people how violent drow could be.

Millwright nodded, and the guard standing nearest to the cage flicked the lightsilk curtain aside. A fluorescent glare flooded the cage, and Ellis' grip on her dagger slipped.

Landon was curled in a ball on the far side of the cage. He had lost weight, and his hair was matted. There was no mattress in his cage. When the senator approached, he howled.

"Lan," Trissa whispered, distraught.

Ellis wanted to slice the throat of the nearest soldier, rip Millwright to shreds, and hold her mother at knife-point until she relinquished every secret she knew.

Senator Chan tentatively spoke through the bars. "Hello?"

"It doesn't understand you, Senator," Millwright reminded her, "but you're quite safe."

His assurances were interrupted by a soldier sprinting down the aisle of tents toward Millwright. Connor pivoted aside a heartbeat before the man would have run into him.

"I need to speak to you, sir," the soldier informed him. Senator Chan raised an eyebrow, and Millwright's face turned beet red. He looked like he would blow a gasket.

"In private, sir," the soldier insisted.

Millwright's eye twitched, but his smile did not falter as he excused himself. Ellis tapped Trissa's shoulder and beckoned for her to follow. Trissa nodded, and the two women crept forward behind the two men.

The soldier brought Millwright behind the tent so that they were blocked from view of the senator and the other employees. The soldier's face was pale as he nervously told Millwright, "Sir, the DRI may be under attack."

CHAPTER TWENTY

Morrissey was on high alert while he and Liza were feeding the spiders. His caution was vindicated when a soldier ran up to them as they were stuffing the final bag of spider chow through the grate. He recognized the young man as the guard who had brought him lunch.

The guard jogged to a halt and panted. He clutched a bundle of fabric to his chest. "Facility-wide Code Indigo."

Liza glanced at the light fixture on the wall, which was dark. "Why hasn't someone sounded the alarm?"

"Millwright's orders. Ix-nay on the iren-say while the senator's here."

Charlie glanced at Liza and raised an eyebrow. Was this her doing? Liza minutely shook her head. Whatever was happening, she had nothing to do with it.

"What do you want us to do?" Morrissey asked.

"Start putting up nets." The man handed Liza the bundle, and Morrissey recognized the fabric's sheen. "These cordon off the exits and arterial halls. Then we search the sections. Start with the zoo exits."

Morrissey didn't understand what the man was saying, but Liza nodded, so he did too. The soldier sprinted away.

Liza hefted the bundle. "Let's go."

She marched down the corridor so fast that Morrissey had to jog to keep up. Beside the door to Millwright's office, they found two soldiers restraining an aggravated pit bull on a makeshift leash.

Morrissey did a double-take. He *knew* that dog. When she saw Morrissey, she stopped barking, and Charlie patted her head. Flower eyed him, then cautiously licked his hand.

This was Ellis' eerily intelligent dog. She had to be the reason for the Code Indigo.

The guard holding Flower's leash narrowed his eyes. "Do you know this dog?"

Morrissey shook his head. "No."

Flower huffed in mild offense and nuzzled his hand. The guard raised an eyebrow. Morrissey sternly eyed Flower, and she huffed again and stopped.

"She doesn't act like Millwright's," the second guard commented.

"They're not usually friendly," Liza agreed. "Sorry we can't help, boys. We gotta go to the zoo." She held up the cloth bundle in explanation and pulled Morrissey away.

When they were out of earshot, she hissed, "What the fuck was that?"

"I think my vigilante friend is in the building," he whispered back.

Liza stopped dead. Charlie slammed into her and nearly knocked the lightsilk out of her arms. *"What?"*

"That was her dog."

She gaped at him. "Why would she bring a *dog* on a *black-ops mission?*"

He threw up his hands. "I don't know, but this is our chance to talk to the senator."

"You lost me."

Charlie stepped in close. "If I'm right, all hell is about to break loose. We can use the chaos to tell the senator what's going on."

"Half the DRI is with her, and they all have guns. *Real* guns."

"*You* have a real gun," Charlie pointed out. Liza's fingers brushed her holster, and he added, "You could give it to me for old time's sake."

"If things go south, we're gonna get shot," Liza grumbled, but she unbuckled the holster. She white-knuckled the leather for a moment, then sighed and handed it over. "I want it on record that I don't like this."

"Neither do I, but I think it's our best shot."

"We are in the *middle* of the *senator's visit,*" Millwright hissed. "What the *fuck* are you *talking about?*" Ellis thought one of the veins pulsing on his forehead would burst and splatter them all with blood.

"Someone re-opened the old subway maintenance entrance, and the armory's gone."

"What do you mean, 'the armory's gone?'"

"There was...an earthquake. That part of the facility collapsed."

Millwright swore under his breath.

An invisible figure came up behind Ellis and merged their shadow magic shrouds. Her father held Claire tightly by the arm.

Ellis narrowed her eyes. The rest of the DRI was on the other side of the tent. Millwright was isolated and vulnerable.

She drew her dagger and leaned forward to whisper in Trissa's ear. "Let me talk to him."

"What? Why?"

"You'll see. Let Claire and me out at the same time. It's for Landon."

Trissa's gaze hardened, and she nodded and lifted her hands. Ellis signaled for her to go ahead, and the air temperature rose a few degrees as she exited the shadows.

Millwright's guard looked over the shorter man's shoulder and blinked in surprise. Millwright turned and frowned. "Claire? Where the hell have you…"

His question died on his lips when he saw Ellis standing behind his partner.

"Mal—" Claire fell silent as Ellis pressed her grandfather's dagger to Claire's throat.

"Do *not* move," Ellis warned her. The moonsteel could cut through sandstone. Severing a spine would be easy. "Do as I say, or Dr. Burton dies." A wave of fear chilled her when she realized that she did not know if she was bluffing.

The soldier's hands drifted toward his gun. Ellis barked, "*Don't*," and he froze.

Millwright looked unconcerned. "What do you want?"

"Clear the zoo and order everyone to leave the facility. Let the people you've kidnapped go."

The paisley-clad man furrowed his brow. "What people?"

Ellis clenched her jaw and contemplated how enjoyable it would be to skin him alive.

In a strangled voice, Claire told him, "She means the MECs, Mal."

Ellis snarled. "Stop fucking *calling* them that. If either of you says that word one more time, she dies."

Millwright considered that. "What will you do afterward?"

"Take my people to safety and bury this place under a Himalayan mass of rock."

"Ah. You must be Ellis." He smiled nonchalantly. "You could have been our most valuable research project, but your mother threw you away. Such a waste. I'm sorry, Claire, but I won't allow what we've built to be destroyed." He glanced at the soldier. "Shoot them."

Claire slumped against Ellis, a rag doll waiting for death. When Ellis dropped her and sprang toward the guard, her mother made a small, surprised noise.

Ellis was inside the guard's reach before he raised his gun. She slashed his trigger hand and yanked the barrel aside as he dropped it, clutching his injured hand. He could bleed to death for all she cared.

In response to Millwright's cries of *"Indigo!"* DRI soldiers poured around the tent, only to slow when they saw Ellis with the rifle.

Ellis glimpsed Claire on her back on the floor. Ellis hoped Millwright's disdain made Claire feel a fraction of the betrayal stewing inside Ellis since her first honest conversation with her father. If Claire was devastated, she might begin to understand how Ellis felt.

Far from the hoped-for despair, her mother's face was blank. Another soldier pushed through the crowd with his rifle raised, and Ellis ran out of time to reflect.

When he pulled the trigger, half the gun dissolved. The rest of the rifle exploded in a ball of fire that left the soldier screaming about his burning hands.

"Smoke out the MECs! Silks up!" Millwright yelled.

An arrow passed through the gap in a petite DRI soldier's body armor, and the woman fell. Ellis followed the flight path to see Mirelle, whose blue face was paler than usual. She looked like she was about to vomit.

A *crack* announced a rain of glittering lightsilk scraps.

"Don't let it touch you!" Ellis shouted to no avail. Trissa popped into visibility beside her with angry red welts on her arms. Behind her, Jorel was in similar shape. Her father remained invisible, having understood the threat well enough to avoid it.

A knot of aides had surrounded the senator and were rushing her away. Two DRI soldiers met them near the exit. Then a guard leveled a handgun at Ellis' chest and pulled the trigger.

Claire screamed, *"No!"* in the background. It was the first true emotion Ellis had witnessed from her all day, but she was too busy catching her breath to think about it.

Ellis tackled the guard as the hot metal slug tumbled from the dent in her crystal-silk shirt. Fire raged through her diaphragm as she knocked the gun out of his hand. Her shirt was nominally bulletproof, but the impact had cracked her sternum.

She punched the man in the head, and he collapsed. Ellis shielded herself with his limp form as she approached Landon's tent. Across the room, another burst of confetti forced two more drow into sight, and they dove behind a tent to avoid a hail of gunfire.

Three soldiers had their guns trained on Ellis, but they were unwilling to shoot their unconscious brother-in-arms. A moment later, their guns dissolved. One guard shrieked and held up a hand missing four fingers. Ellis forced herself not to look at the exposed bone.

The lightsilk had fallen back across the bars of Landon's cage. Ellis prepared for the worst as she hefted the senseless guard over her shoulder and reached for it.

Before she could touch the fabric, Claire stopped her. "Let me."

She yanked the lightsilk off the cage. Curled up in a ball on the other side of the cage, Landon did not twitch. His glassy eyes stared at nothing.

Ellis tasted bile. Someone would pay for this.

Connor ran up beside her. "Cover me. I'll break through the bars." He had avoided the lightsilk. Thank the Mother Beneath that *someone* still had shadow magic.

Ellis dropped the unconscious guard beside the cage and sank into a defensive stance. Two other soldiers approached with confetti guns raised rather than firearms. They were eyeing Connor, whom they had identified as the main threat.

"Not so fast, assholes!" Ellis leaped forward and kicked the confetti gun out of one soldier's hand. The other man fired, but Ellis took the brunt of the blast. It burned like hell, but none of the scraps of fabric reached her father.

She heard Connor speaking gently behind her. "*Landon. Landon, can you hear me?*"

Ellis had rarely heard her father afraid, and it filled her with rage. *I will* kill *Malcolm Millwright.*

She became a blur as she deked around tents and bounded over downed soldiers. She trusted any shrouded drow to dodge. How hard could it be to spot a fucking *paisley lab coat?*

Ellis spotted a flash of the psychedelic fabric at the edge of the cavern. Millwright was huddled behind a stack of packing crates, guarded by two soldiers. Ellis unsheathed her dagger and adjusted her grip. If his head popped up again, she would throw the knife.

She did not get the chance. Millwright saw her approach and shouted at the guards, but she derived no pleasure from his cowardly fear since she had an assault rifle pointed at her chest. Crystal silk would not save her from an automatic weapon.

A familiar voice boomed through the cavern. "*Stop!*"

The guard with his rifle trained on Ellis glanced over her shoulder, and miraculously, he obeyed. When Ellis turned, she understood why.

Charlie Morrissey had a handgun pointed at Senator Arden Chan's head. Fear simmered in her eyes, but she was outwardly calm.

"*Who gave you a gun?*" Millwright shrieked. The guard in front of him surreptitiously wiped spit off the back of his neck.

Liza stepped up beside him. "I did."

Morrissey kept his gun trained on the senator, but his gaze was riveted on Millwright. "I apologize for this, Senator, but since you're here to assess this facility, I wanted to ensure that you saw the full picture."

"I might find active listening easier without a gun pointed at my head," the senator coolly informed him.

"I sympathize, but we all have obstacles to overcome."

Charlie's calm voice made Ellis feel like her stomach was turning inside out. She had not realized how much she had missed him over the past few days. His gaze flicked to her, and a relieved smile crossed his face.

What was his game? Did he want Ellis to rescue the senator? Should she let another drow rescue the woman? She twitched an eyebrow inquisitively, but before she could guess, Charlie took the reins.

"There's someone I'd like you to meet, Senator Chan, but Millwright's men need to drop their weapons first."

Chan nodded at the two soldiers with Millwright. "If you please, gentlemen."

"Don't you dare!" Millwright spat.

Charlie was unperturbed. "See it my way, Dr. Millwright." His tone was very reasonable for a man with a hostage. "The DRI has flown under the radar for a long time, but there are things even you can't cover up. If a United States senator dies on your watch, you're done. Even *if* the DRI stayed open, your head would be the first in line for the chopping block, possibly literally. They'd want someone to pin it on."

Thick, oppressive silence filled the cavern. The air by Ellis' neck chilled, and Trissa whispered, "Should I stop the hostage-taker?"

"Not yet," Ellis whispered. If Morrissey's betrayal had been genuine, he would not have attacked the senator.

"Stand down," Millwright ordered through gritted teeth. His men slowly complied.

Liza strolled over to collect their weapons and paused beside Ellis on the way back. "Little help?" she murmured.

"What's your plan?" Ellis whispered.

Consternation flashed over Liza's face. *Uh-oh.* Maybe there was no plan. Charlie was apparently improvising. *No one's shooting at each other, so I guess it's working.*

Ellis acquired a dart gun and two knives as she stripped the remaining soldiers of their weapons. Then she waved Frella and Welton over.

The senator gasped and stumbled. Charlie caught and steadied her. At first, Ellis thought Chan might be attempting to escape. Then she realized that the senator was gaping at the young drow who had dropped their shrouds.

Charlie smiled ruefully. "Welcome to the club, Senator. You'll get used to it…sort of."

Her eyes were wide. "They have weapons."

Ellis crossed her arms. "We sure do. If Dr. Shithead makes a wrong move, you'll see us use them."

She stalked over to Millwright and hauled him out from behind the crates. Ellis was tempted to shatter his stupid human humerus—it would not be difficult—but she forced herself to remain calm. She would let Morrissey do his thing before she thought about revenge.

The senator narrowed her eyes, and curiosity overshadowed her fear. "What do you mean, 'us?'"

Ellis paused, fumbling for a sophisticated speech about the importance of her drow heritage and her connection to the homestead and being a child of two worlds, then realized few knew about her parentage. The drow did, and Morrissey had probably guessed, but how many people in the DRI knew? What if the senator identified her as a national security threat? Maybe it was better to stay quiet.

Morrissey saved her. "She means the people who have worked to bring you the truth."

Ellis nodded in relief.

"Don't trust her! She's a MEC!" Millwright exclaimed as he struggled in vain to escape Ellis' vise grip.

Chan raised an eyebrow. "You told me the MECs couldn't talk."

Millwright squirmed harder. Ellis was thrilled to use that as an excuse to tighten her grip and bruise his weaselly arm.

"I assure you that we are perfectly capable of speech." The deep male voice emanated from the air beside Ellis, and her father popped into view a moment later. Claire stood uneasily beside him. Connor held her upper arm as Ellis held Millwright's.

Millwright sighed when he saw Claire. The noise was barely audible, but Ellis felt his muscles relax. He might be an evil bastard, but he cared about her mother.

Then he frowned. *"Connor?"*

Connor tugged Claire forward. He regarded Millwright as though he were a particularly ugly and unpalatable species of cavefish. It was easy to forget that they had known each other decades ago.

Chan eyed Connor. "Who are you?" She no longer seemed bothered by the gun Morrissey kept trained on her back, although Ellis doubted she had forgotten it was there.

Connor's voice was pure ice. "I believe the DRI's designation for me was 'Subject Zero.'" Claire flinched.

The senator looked at the three. "Director Millwright, I was under the impression that the DRI was an animal testing facility. I wasn't aware you were experimenting with human subjects."

"They're not human!" Millwright protested.

"They certainly haven't been treated with human *dignity*," Morrissey spat, and disgust curdled the senator's face. She seemed to agree.

"The director's technically correct," Claire quietly, then coldly informed her, "They're *not* human. They're genetically distinct."

"You're Dr. Burton. Millwright claimed you were ill."

"He was mistaken."

Morrissey nudged the senator toward Landon's cage. "Senator, you need to see what this place does."

Chan approached. She took in the details of the drow who were now visible around her: the details of their silk clothing, the workmanship of their bows, and, of course, the myriad shades of their skin.

Ellis manhandled Millwright toward Morrissey and Chan. Connor followed with Claire. Inside the cage, Trissa was crouched beside Landon, who had not yet acknowledged her.

Morrissey started when he saw Trissa. "You owe me a car roof!"

Senator Chan blinked. "What?"

"Long story."

Trissa eyed Morrissey. "Are you *sure* I can't take him out, Ellis?"

Charlie opened his mouth to object, but Ellis shook her head. "He's with us. I think."

"I'm certainly not with the DRI. I would never work for people who would do *that* to someone." Morrissey gestured at Landon.

Her brother was catatonic. Did he even understand what they were saying? Ellis remembered her short stay in these cages. "MECs don't talk," they had told her. Then they had electrified the floor.

Pity and disgust warred on Chan's face as she inspected the cage and its occupant. Ellis' gorge rose, and she could not stomach it any longer. She flung Millwright aside and stepped between Senator Chan and her brother.

"Stop it!" Her voice broke. "He's a person, not a freak for you to ogle!"

Embarrassed, Chan took a half-step back. She ran into Morrissey's gun and flinched.

"She needs to see what they've done, Ellis," Morrissey told her. The compassion in his voice made her want to sob.

Connor echoed him. "Yes. She *does* need to see what they've done." Ellis did not think he was talking about the senator, given that his long purple fingers were digging into Claire's upper arm.

Millwright crawled away across the floor, and Ellis let him go. The drow controlled the cavern and all the weapons. She would have fun recapturing him in a few minutes. Maybe he would resist, and she could kick him in the face.

Trissa threw the oppressive crowd the kind of disapproving look only an infirmarian could muster. She uncorked a small glass bottle and held it to Landon's lips. "Lan, will you please drink the rustcap juice?" He flinched away, and her eyes glistened with tears.

She recorked the bottle and carefully stowed it in her bag. Then, faster than Ellis could track, she was holding a knife to Claire's neck. "You know what happens if I cut your carotid," she growled. "What did you *do* to him?"

Ellis was unsure what a carotid was, but her mother's face went white, so she did. Connor seemed disinclined to interfere. It had taken Ellis two decades to find her mother, and now she would watch Claire's throat sliced open in front of her. "Trissa, please don't kill her," she begged.

Claire's face was blank. "I deserve it."

"You deserve much *worse*," Trissa hissed. "Will you die a coward, or will you tell me what you've *done* so I can *help* him?"

"They're conditioned not to talk." A young man stepped forward. Roughly Ellis' age, he wore a DRI uniform. Mirelle covered him, alert for attacks or escape attempts.

Morrissey nodded at the guard. "Thanks for the lunch."

The guard nodded back. Ellis was confused but decided to let the interaction play out. The young guard went on. "The director told us that the MECs couldn't talk, not truly. He told us they were like parrots. You know, mimicking human sounds. He said it was important that none of them made any noise during the senator's visit, so…he upped the amperage and told us to reinforce the conditioning."

"You mean torture," Trissa snapped.

The guard said nothing, but he blushed. The senator made a disgusted noise. Landon shivered.

"We have to get him out of here," Ellis told Trissa. "To a place where he doesn't think he will be electrocuted if he speaks." She looked at Chan and drew a deep breath. "Senator, my...Landon's not the only captive. There are other drow."

Chan frowned. "Drow?"

"What these people call 'MECs.'" The word was sour in her mouth.

Charlie spoke up. "We'll find them."

It was grim work. They went from cage to cage, allowing Claire and the helpful guard to pull down the lightsilk curtains. The facility was equipped for many more drow than it currently held. Ellis was unsure of why. That was a question for another day.

They found two men and one woman, as Claire had promised—young outcasts who had disappeared over the past few years. The drow had assumed they had gone to live in the city or traveled to other dark elf communities, and no one had looked for them.

The young guard handed Ellis his keys. When she opened the first cage, the drow inside attacked her in terror. He pummeled her and bit her twice. The other drow were so startled that they did nothing.

Ellis would have lost the fight if Liza had not shot the drow with a dart containing a clear, viscous liquid. When Ellis turned on the detective in anger, Liza held up her hands to placate her.

"You need to get your people out of here. You can't do that if they kill you."

Ellis sighed. Her guts twisted at the sight of the

malnourished figure on the floor. Liza was right. Healing would not happen in the zoo.

She discussed the logistics with Connor and Trissa. The DRI had two wheeled stretchers, which were not sufficient for all four drow. So far, Landon had not been violent, but that could change. He was not ready to walk.

Connor sliced iron bars from a cage, and Ulivi knotted crystal silk rope into a rough sling to hang between them. The senator watched in amazement.

While Connor and Trissa tested the makeshift stretcher, Mirelle approached with a young DRI guard, whom she nudged toward Ellis. When her fingers made contact with the lightsilk, she winced. "He wanted to talk to the senator."

It took Ellis a second to place the soldier. He was the one she had saved in the apartment building. She hoped he was not about to punish her for saving his life.

The senator tilted her head. "Yes?"

"Senator, you should know that Millwright is holding a prisoner in his office."

"What?" Chan was shocked. "Another...what did you call them?" She glanced at Ellis.

"Drow, or dark elves," Ellis replied.

The senator turned back to the soldier. "Is it another drow?" Ellis' estimation of the woman rose by a mile.

The soldier shook his head. "It's a human. I saw him while I was cleaning the office one night."

"And you did not report it?"

"Report to who?" The kid was mystified.

Chan huffed. "The director has some explaining to do."

Tracking Millwright was not as much fun as Ellis had

hoped. She found him cowering in a lump under a lightsilk curtain. She yanked him out by the ankle and marched him back to the group.

Chan eyed Millwright, then glanced at Morrissey over her shoulder. "I'm unarmed, and you have the upper hand. Perhaps you don't need to point that thing directly at my spine."

Charlie raised an eyebrow at Ellis, who shrugged. Charlie lowered the gun.

A practiced smile bloomed on Chan's face. "Lead the way, young man."

CHAPTER TWENTY-ONE

The drow herded the remaining DRI soldiers into three tents. Jorel, Rollo, and a drow whose name Ellis had not caught stayed in case someone else showed up with a key, but Ellis doubted they would have any problems.

She was sorely tempted to shock them before she left, but she decided to take the high road. She *did* show Jorel the button, however. "In case anyone causes trouble." She glared through the bars, then smiled insincerely. "If you're good, I'll bring you kibbles."

Ellis set out with the others to rescue Millwright's final captive. Several drow whose shadow magic had not been burned away scouted ahead. Lightsilk nets had been stretched across many of the halls, but they found a round-about route.

They ran into two soldiers arguing about how to tie a bowline, and the men surrendered. As a drow marched them to the zoo, Ellis cheerfully called after them, "The rabbit goes through the hole, around the tree, and back through the hole!" before gingerly stepping over their abandoned net.

Millwright's office was locked by a handprint scanner beside the door.

Ellis poked him. "Open it."

"No," Millwright snapped petulantly. The bright lab coat, which had seemed eccentric, now seemed pathetic.

Ellis scowled. "Put your hand on the scanner, or I'll cut it off and do it myself."

Mirelle marched Millwright to the door. He lifted his hand to the scanner, but rather than laying it flat, he tapped in a code. A heavy metallic *thud* rang out.

Millwright sneered. "It's now deadbolted. It can't be opened for twenty-four hours."

Charlie groaned. "Maybe it's better that way. He has a loose cobra in there."

Ellis' heart skipped a beat. All this time, she had wondered where Percy had gone. If the snake was still alive, Percy was with him. "Percy might be in there! We have to open it!"

Connor stepped forward. "Allow me."

Her father gestured, and the edges of the door dissolved. It was delicate, precise shadow magic work.

"You're showing off," Ellis muttered. She smiled when his lips quirked up.

Connor turned a baleful stare on Millwright as he placed a finger against the door and pushed. It fell with a resounding *thump.*

The room beyond was only lit with the faint glow of emergency lights. Ellis halted her instinctive entry when a whisper of movement caught her eye.

Millwright cackled as the king cobra slithered toward them. Mirelle raised her bow, but Ellis raised a hand. "Don't hurt it if you don't have to. It's Percy's."

"Not anymore, it's not," Millwright snarled. "It's mine!"

Ellis trusted Percy. Animals he could not win over were rare. On the other hand, a massive king cobra was approaching her ankles at a surprising speed.

Her primeval fear won out. She shouted for everyone to back up, and they obeyed with alacrity—all except for Millwright, who took a step *toward* the snake. Welton, holding the director's wrists, stumbled forward with him.

Fortunately, the snake halted its rapid advance when Millwright did. The front third of its body rose off the concrete floor in a lithe curve.

In profile, Ellis realized why Millwright seemed familiar. He looked like Percy. The details did not match—Malcolm's eyebrows were thin, and he lacked Percy's smile lines—but the way he focused on the snake was identical.

The main difference was in the eyes. Where Percy was interested and empathetic when he communicated with animals, Millwright was heartless and cold.

"You're talking to the cobra," Ellis murmured. "You're the reason Ron Jackson killed the fish and the rat."

A cruel smile played on Millwright's lips. "That idiot *dangerously* overestimated his abilities. He thought if he knocked off a few lousy goldfish, I wouldn't find out about his extracurricular activities. He was wrong."

"Call the snake off," Ellis told him.

Millwright sickeningly chortled. "Whatever do you mean? It's a wild animal."

He locked gazes with the cobra again. Then, its beady

black gaze flicked in Ellis' direction. Two seconds passed in silence before the snake looped back into the office.

Millwright hissed. The cobra whipped back around and bared its fangs. Venom glistened on the white points.

It looked...*conflicted.* Could a snake *be* conflicted? Ellis assumed its instincts were straightforward: slither, bite, or swallow.

It focused on Ellis and swayed. She stumbled away, and Welton wrenched Millwright back, but they were too slow. The snake shot forward and buried its fangs in Malcolm Millwright's ankle.

Welton dropped Millwright like a nightmare node and unsheathed his dagger, but the cobra lazily detached its fangs from the director and slithered into the office, then curled around its branch.

Ellis darted into the office and shouted, *"Percy!"* The room was not large. Underground, real estate was at a premium. Percy was nowhere to be seen.

"He's behind the painting, ma'am," the quiet guard from earlier informed her.

Ellis grabbed the creepy oil painting. The backs of her fingers burned, and she leaped away, shaking her hands. The wall behind the painting was covered in gauzy light-silk. In the dim light, she had mistaken it for textured wallpaper.

She *carefully* hoisted the painting down, revealing the glass enclosure. Thanks to her drow night vision, she could make out Percy sitting as far as possible from an uneaten hamburger.

Percy was gaunt and exhausted. He stared at Ellis as though he could not believe she was real, then crawled to the glass and flattened his hands on it. He spoke, but Ellis heard nothing. The glass was soundproof.

Connor came up beside her, lifting his hands to cut through the glass with shadow magic. Ellis stopped him and pointed out the lightsilk covering. Claire had followed him in and was staring at Percy in the cramped terrarium in dismay.

"How do I open this?" Ellis demanded.

"I don't know," Claire replied. "I didn't realize Mal had…"

Ellis ignored the rest of her mother's awkward attempt at an explanation and stalked back to Millwright. He was leaning on the wall in the corridor, clutching his ankle. He looked clammy and pale, and his breathing was ragged.

"Antivenin," he gasped. "In the nutrition lab."

She nudged him with her boot. "What's the magic word?"

"I'll die without it."

"Oh, *no*." Ellis drew the syllables out with languid disinterest. "What a *shame*."

"Give me the antivenin, and I'll tell you how to open the enclosure."

Ellis shivered at the word. She wanted nothing more than to watch Malcolm lose control of his limbs as the bite went necrotic, but she could not leave Percy. "Fine. Tell me."

"Antivenin first."

"No. After Percy's out, Welton will take you to the lab. You have my word."

Millwright crossed his arms and clamped his mouth

shut, but his mulishness was interrupted by a gasp of pain as his eyelid spasmed.

Ellis tapped her foot. "Unlike the idiots you've hitched your wagon to, I'm a woman of my word. If you want to live, all you have to do is believe me."

Millwright glowered. The color was draining from his skin, but impending death had made him no less of an asshole. His lip twitched, and he growled. "A button under my desk opens a panel in the maintenance closet next door."

Ellis ran in, eyeing the cobra in the corner as she fell to her knees behind the mahogany desk. "Good boy?" she ventured. The snake hissed in response.

She threw open the desk drawer. She found no secret buttons, but the brass shield of Charlie's badge gleamed. She pocketed it, then crawled beneath the desk and ran her hands over the underside. She found a button no bigger than her pinky nail.

She hesitated. It might fire poison darts or trigger a trapdoor into an abyss.

He probably accidentally hits it with his knee all the time. It won't kill you.

She drew a deep breath and pressed the button.

A low rumble sounded behind her. Percy ignored it. He was smiling at the king cobra in the corner, looking unhinged.

Some things I'll never understand.

When Ellis returned to the corridor, Connor was preparing to dissolve the maintenance closet's door. She tried the handle, and it was unlocked.

Connor blushed. "Oh."

181

Ellis snickered. "You might consider taking the easy way on occasion."

Metal shelves hid a silver panel on the back wall of the closet. They pushed the shelves aside and found that the panel was padlocked shut.

"Can I show off now?" Connor mildly asked.

"Be my guest."

After the padlock dissolved, she yanked the door open. "Percy!"

Percy was still kneeling on the floor. When he saw her, he smiled wearily. "Ellis. I knew the threads of Fate would pull you back."

"I'm here." She stepped back to allow him to come out. The space was not big enough for two.

Percy shakily stood and leaned on the glass as he walked to the door. He collapsed like an accordion after crossing the threshold. Ellis caught him.

He spoke into her shoulder. "I take it you've met my brother."

Ellis' stomach swooped as the similarities between Percy Rawlings and Malcolm Millwright became crystal clear. "Millwright is your *brother?*"

Her father loomed in the doorway. "Are you certain this man is trustworthy?"

Ellis glared. "Millwright's been keeping him in a *cage.*" Connor's expression did not change. Ellis rolled her eyes. "Yes, he's trustworthy. Even if he wasn't, I'm right here, and he's too weak to pose a threat."

"Don't underestimate me." Percy attempted to stand on his own but ended up crashing into the metal shelves.

Buckets of cleaning supplies rattled and sloshed, and Connor's hand shot out to steady the rack.

Percy sheepishly smiled. "Point taken."

Connor raised an eyebrow, then turned to Ellis. "Do you intend to administer the antivenin to Millwright?"

"Yes. Welton can take him."

Connor nodded and left. Morrissey took his place a moment and smiled at Percy. "Hey, Percy. I'm glad you're all right."

A bright smile appeared on Percy's face. "Detective! Back on the side of good, eh? I hoped you'd come around."

"It's not 'Detective' anymore. Just Charlie."

Liza appeared behind Charlie and gasped. "Oh, my God. Is that the bank robber?"

Percy grumbled. "I'm a hacker and a pet psychic. I've had a lot of jobs. Bank robber is *way* down the list."

"You're a wanted fugitive," Liza accused.

"It's nice to be wanted," Percy cheerfully agreed.

"When they arrest me for kidnapping a senator, we can share a cell at San Quentin," Morrissey commented.

"While I welcome your friendship, Detect…er, *Charlie*, I am unwilling to commit to incarceration at this moment."

Ellis frowned at Percy. "Did you know your brother was with the DRI? How did I not know you had a brother?"

Percy reached down and rubbed his calf. Ellis was about to repeat the question when he replied, "I suspected Mal might be here. You have to understand, girlie. I haven't seen him in two decades, but when we encountered those spiders, I thought his icy hand might be pulling their strings."

"How did you know?"

"We have the same abilities, or 'demonic afflictions,' as our mother called them. However, we use them to *very* different ends. My approach is collaborative. He prefers fear and pain."

Ellis had to agree that "fear and pain" succinctly described her experiences with the DRI.

Percy let his head fall back against the shelf. "We grew up in hardscrabble Appalachia. Common parlance termed us hillbillies. Our mother abandoned us as boys, under the misapprehension that our way with animals was inherently evil."

His tone was light, but Ellis felt the ache beneath. They had not discussed their respective childhoods. Perhaps growing up without a mother was the reason she and Percy had developed such a strong bond.

Ellis spotted the hamburger in the enclosure. "Was he feeding you meat?"

Percy nodded. "I woulda eaten it eventually. I don't think I'm better than lions and tigers. I just didn't want to see the smug satisfaction on my brother's face."

His words tumbled out in a semi-coherent ramble. "Our dad used to take us hunting. I tried to wriggle out of it, but Pa insisted. Mal loved it. He'd listen to the nearby game—you know, with his mind. Terribly unsportsmanlike, but they never came home empty-handed.

"Pa only wanted to fill our freezer, but Mal liked killing. He'd coax rabbits out of their holes so he could shoot them. Paw let me stop going when he realized I was countering Mal's moves by scaring away anything he lured out.

"I left home when I was seventeen, and I swore I would

never eat meat again. Speaking of which, do you happen to have any food on you?"

Ellis found a piece of tunnel bar in her pocket and handed it over, along with a bottle of water. Percy gratefully ate it between sips of water.

She put a gentle hand on his shoulder. "You changed your name?"

Percy nodded. "I wanted Mal to have to work for it if he wanted to track me down. Now it turns out he was under my feet the whole time." He chuckled.

"Once in a while, I'd meet an animal that had gone rotten, and I'd have an inkling that he was in the city. I convinced myself I was being paranoid." He looked out of the closet. "Is he all right?"

Only Percy would care about his bastard of a brother. The man was too good for this world. "The cobra bit him," Ellis replied. "He stocks antivenin. He'll probably be okay."

Percy grinned. "I *knew* Prickles was on the side of righteousness. The Bible does snakes dirty, you know. They're beautiful animals."

He glanced at Charlie and Liza. "Are you going to arrest me?"

"I'm not a detective anymore, remember?" Charlie replied. They looked too exhausted to arrest anyone.

Ellis retrieved his badge from her pocket and handed it to him. "Don't be so sure."

His face fell. "I don't deserve it. Ellis, I joined the DRI to save my skin."

"Then you kidnapped a senator."

She had meant it positively, but Charlie's expression

darkened. "That *definitely* means I won't be a cop for much longer. Arresting Percy isn't much of a final hurrah."

Liza snorted. "Are you kidding me? He's on the FBI's Most Wanted list. You'd be the envy of the department. You might even get a medal."

Ellis slipped her arm under Percy's and motioned the detectives out of the supply closet. "You can consider your career goals later. What are we going to do with the senator?"

"If you want me to shut down the DRI, you'll have to let me live," Chan coolly replied. She was leaning on the wall outside the supply closet, heels in hand. Two drow were guarding her, and she pointed a heel at them. "Your friends aren't very talkative."

Ellis raised an eyebrow. "After what you've seen today, can you blame them?"

Chan appeared to consider the question.

The senator posed a problem, but before Ellis could find a solution, Connor arrived. "Welton and Millwright have been gone too long."

Ellis frowned. "Where'd they go?"

"Through the door in the back of his office."

Morrissey tilted his head. "Into the animal lab?"

"You let Mal near *animals?*" Panic laced Percy's voice. "Ellis, we need to go. Bring me."

Ellis bit her lip. "Charlie, Liza, stay with the senator. We'll handle Millwright."

Charlie nodded. "It's a long corridor. Zero cover, floor-to-ceiling cages. Be safe."

"Sounds lovely." She helped Percy toward the office. "You up for cobra-wrangling?"

Percy waved at the snake on their way by. "I wouldn't worry. Prickles wants to bask."

"Tell him he can bask from a distance," Ellis muttered.

The snake did not twitch as they approached the thick metal door.

"I can feel them," Percy murmured after he laid a palm flat against the door. "They're frightened. Give them a wide berth."

Ellis nodded. "Dad, you're in charge of shadow magic."

"What will you do?" her father asked.

She shrugged. "What I'm best at, which is kicking stuff. Let's stop that son of a bitch."

CHAPTER TWENTY-TWO

The lab was silent. The light from the office illuminated only the first few feet of the narrow room and did nothing to reveal the animals, who huddled unmoving against the walls. Ellis tried the switch beside the door, but it did nothing.

Percy drew a shaky breath and whispered, "They're so scared."

Ellis, Percy, and Connor crept down the aisle in single file. It was only forty feet long, but it felt like a hundred. The door closed behind Connor with a menacing *snick*.

Ellis stopped dead, and Percy stumbled into her back. "Please tell me that didn't lock."

Connor tried the handle. "It did. Shall I blast it open?"

Before Ellis could respond, the far door opened, and the overhead lights flickered on.

Malcolm Millwright stood on the threshold. The gaudy paisley of his lab coat was splattered with blood. "It's amazing what kind of distraction an angry guinea pig can provide."

"Where's Welton?" Ellis demanded.

Millwright smiled, then brought a drow dagger from behind his back and wiped it on the hem of his lab coat. "I've taken blood samples from many MECs, but rarely so imprecisely. A shame, but now I can provide my test subjects with a veritable tasting flight of fresh meat."

Ellis' upper lip curled, and she launched into a sprint.

"*Ellis, don't!*" Percy shouted.

His warning came too late. Ellis caught the gleam of the unlatched cage door halfway down the hall as Millwright laughed and yelled, "*Now!*"

Oh, shit.

Every cage door banged open, and claws scraped on concrete. Fur and scales shone as Millwright's subjects poured into the narrow passage.

A visceral snarl pierced the feral symphony as a jaguar padded out of its cage. A porcupine waddled in front of it, and the jaguar idly swiped it away before turning to face Ellis.

Ellis wrenched Landon's dagger from her belt, but Connor roughly pushed her behind him. He raised his hands, but his spell was thrown off when Percy desperately yanked his sleeve. A twelve-foot hole appeared in the ceiling, baring live wires that sparked like firecrackers.

"*Don't hurt them! It's not their fault!*" Percy's shout was barely audible.

He was right, but that was cold comfort when you were facing a cat the size of a Harley-Davidson. Connor did not bother arguing. He clenched his fists and raised them again.

Percy grabbed Connor's arm and begged, *"Wait!* I can stop them!"

Her father paused at the expression on Percy's face. "You have ten seconds."

The jaguar prowled toward them. Its ribs were visible under its gleaming fur, but it appeared to be in no hurry. Ellis raised her dagger uncertainly. If the jaguar attacked, it would be as useful as a cocktail pick.

Percy stepped in front of Connor and sank to one knee. The jaguar hesitated, then sank to its haunches. Its tail flicked, and it licked its paw.

Percy deliberately looked at the floor in front of the jaguar. "I know you're scared and underfed, but trust me, we're not worth eating. I'm as starved as you, and the small one's better with that dagger than she looks."

The jaguar ceased grooming its paw. With a low growl, it extended its claws.

Percy's voice was thick with fear, but he kept his words even. "I happen to have insider information regarding the location of an uneaten hamburger. If you'd be so kind as to stand down, I'd be happy to point you to it."

The jaguar eyed Percy. Ellis could figure out its train of thought. Percy might have been skinny, but he was a lot bigger than a hamburger.

Millwright's eye twitched as he stalked toward the jaguar. *"Kill them,"* he ordered.

The jaguar flinched. A wave of sympathy overrode Ellis' sense of self-preservation, and she pointed her dagger at Millwright.

The big cat's hackles rose. Percy drew back, and Ellis

realized their psychic link had broken. The jaguar roared and raised a paw.

Bolstered by the jaguar's display of aggression, a Komodo dragon lumbered toward them, although it paused to snarl at a large, heavy blue-and-black bird—a cassowary if Ellis was not mistaken. She had caught part of a nature documentary that had asserted that cassowaries were the most dangerous birds on the planet. They regularly killed people.

Ellis had broken the first and most important law of the jungle, which was, "Don't menace a bunch of hungry, frightened animals."

The jaguar's back legs tensed. Ellis' heart skipped a beat, and for a moment, she was certain her death was imminent.

A silver blur exploded from the cage beside her and leaped onto the jaguar's back with a ferocious growl.

"Flower!" Percy cheerfully exclaimed.

Ellis took the opportunity to sprint toward Millwright. The Komodo dragon lifted its head and opened its maw full of can-opener teeth, but Ellis vaulted over the reptile. The movement startled the cassowary, and its talon's swipe missed her by a foot.

She landed and kept running. Millwright's skin was pale and mottling an ironic purple, but he ran for the door. Ellis kicked him in the spine. It was nice to go back to basics.

"Help me!" he screamed. The cassowary shrieked but did not look over. It was focused on Percy, who had stretched his arms out to his sides, palms up. A barn owl perched on his shoulder, and Flower lay on the floor beside him.

"Attack! *Attack!*" Millwright's screeches seemed louder now that the cacophony was lessening.

The jaguar licked Percy's outstretched hand. Percy smiled. "Oh, ho! If you keep flattering me, you'll wind up with more cheeseburgers than you can handle, my friend."

Millwright made an exasperated noise in the back of his throat and weakly attempted to grapple with Ellis, who barely had to pay attention to bat away his weak punches. She lifted him by the lapels of his stupid lab coat and was about to fling him into the nearest cage when Percy called to her. "Get him out of here, Ellis! They're all still scared of him!"

Ellis briefly entertained a fantasy of throwing Millwright into the middle of the room and locking the doors on both ends. If they were all as underfed as that jaguar, nature would heal itself before long.

Unfortunately, the premise of this rescue mission was that she was better than that. Revenge might be sweet, but she was here for boring nutritional *justice*.

"Are you sure you have this under control?" she asked.

"After you leave, I will!" Percy assured her. He was far too calm, given that he was within tasting range of a two-hundred-pound jaguar.

Ellis decided to trust him. She hauled Millwright through the door, then closed it. The din immediately ceased, which meant the lab was soundproofed.

She spotted a pile of kibble on the industrial counter, and revulsion curled her gut. An orange-and-white guinea pig was devouring the food.

"I wouldn't go near it if I was you," Millwright advised.

"I should stick you in a cage and make *you* eat that shit," she snarled. Her boot splashed on her next step, and she swore when she looked down and saw blood—and Welton.

The drow moaned, then gasped. "Ellis?"

Ellis scowled. She could not let Millwright go *again*, but she could not leave her brother-in-arms on the ground, either.

She picked up the pace, ignoring the bloody boot prints she left behind. "I'll send help. Wait here."

"I couldn't leave if I tried," Welton rasped.

Stepping into the corridor, Ellis heard tense voices around the corner. Something was wrong. She clamped a hand over Millwright's mouth before he could yell, then inched down the hall and peered around the corner.

A DRI soldier had an automatic rifle trained on Mirelle, who was struggling under a lightsilk net. Her skin was crisscrossed with burns.

Ellis ducked back at the sound of rapid footsteps from the other direction, followed by Claire yelling, *"Stop! Stand down!"* Ellis winced. They must have missed a group of soldiers.

"I can't do that, ma'am," the soldier replied. "We've been infiltrated, and I need to protect the senator. Millwright told us we couldn't trust you, Doc."

"You spoke to Millwright?" Chan's voice. *Oh, Mother Beneath.*

At the sound of his name, Millwright desperately flung himself forward and yelled, *"Help!"* Ellis was caught off-guard, and they tumbled into a heap.

She scrambled upright, dragging Millwright with her as a human shield. He was so much shorter that Ellis had to bend her knees to shield herself properly. It was annoying, but not as annoying as gunshot wounds.

Millwright blubbered, *"Don't shoot!"*

Senator Chan stepped forward a few paces. "Let him go."

"You've seen what he does here," Ellis challenged her. "How can you be on his side?"

"Choosing between the DRI and a cell of foreign guerillas isn't much of a choice."

"Foreign?" Ellis scoffed. "We were all born in or *near* LA. You were born in Massachusetts!"

Chan raised an eyebrow. "You're familiar with my career?"

Ellis shrugged. "I've seen the attack ads." She realized she had revealed important information about the homestead's location. *Shit.* Ellis was running out of options.

She sighed. "I'll turn myself in."

Claire gaped. *"What?"*

"Let everyone else go, and I'll surrender." It was the only way Ellis could think of to save her people. "I'll cooperate. You can keep me in a cage and feed me kibbles and shock me, but only if you let the rest of the drow leave."

Mild disgust crossed Chan's face at the mention of electroshock and kibbles. Claire was apoplectic.

"Ellis, you *can't!"*

Ellis laughed humorlessly. "If it's good enough for Landon, why isn't it good enough for me?" She would gladly sacrifice herself to save her family. Did Claire still count? After what she had learned today, she was no longer sure.

She hoped she would not have to follow through on the

surrender. Her father and Percy might still come through. *When in doubt, stall for time.*

A noise like rain on a tin roof washed into the corridor. It took a moment before Ellis realized they were too far underground to hear rain. "What is that?"

Millwright, still in her grip, laughed. The sick cackling crescendoed as the tapping swelled into thunder. "I released all the safeties!"

Oh, shit.

"Cave spiders!" Ellis screamed as the first black shape dropped onto Senator Chan from a nearby vent. The arachnids poured into the corridor from every opening as the human knocked the spider off her face.

Ellis dropped Millwright and backed toward the others, dagger raised. "We have to work together!"

"Don't come any clo—" The soldier's warning turned into a scream. Ellis risked glancing back and saw the man on the floor with a talon piercing his shoulder, holding him down as the creature sank its fangs into his arm.

Then a spider was on *her.* She batted a talon-tipped leg away and twisted out of reach of the incoming bite. It screeched, and she kicked it across the floor.

Ellis flipped her dagger around to hold it by its point, then let fly. The dagger spun end over end and plunged to the hilt into the spider's abdomen. Goo splattered the floor.

Another spider dropped onto her shoulder, cutting her celebration short, and now she had no weapon. That had been an oversight.

Gunfire cut through the endless clicking of claws. The

DRI soldiers had given up on holding the drow at gunpoint and turned on the eight-legged attackers.

Ellis pulled a lightsilk net off a cowering drow, ignoring the burning on her hands as she flung it at the nearest cave spiders. Their legs waved through the holes in the net as the creatures struggled, but she had entangled three.

Three more crawled over the tangled ball, then fired webs from their spinnerets at Ellis.

"Get down!" Connor shouted from behind her. Ellis dropped and tried not to think about spider guts on her jumpsuit. Three arrows whistled overhead and hit their marks with solid, wet *thuds.*

Flower barked, and Ellis could have cried in relief. She and Percy had made it out.

Then she heard a low keening. At first, Ellis thought it was coming from the spiders. Her jaw dropped when she discovered its true source.

Percy was riding Flower like a surfboard, one foot on her shoulders and the other on her haunches. His eyes were pure white, his arms were outstretched, and his head was tilted back as the unearthly wail emanated from his open mouth.

It was soothing, reminding her of a singing bowl. Her breathing slowed, and she relaxed. She could have basked in the drone forever.

The spiders calmed down as well. They were still alive, but they were now inspecting their victims with curiosity rather than ill will. Even Millwright wore an insipid smile, although cruelty still lurked in his eyes.

The paisley-bedecked madman struggled to his feet.

Fighting Percy's siren song, he took faltering steps toward his brother. "You bastard!"

Ellis had to stop him, but she was very comfortable, and the nice spider entrails cushioned her from the nasty concrete. Maybe she would stop Millwright after a nap.

She let her head drop to the floor, only to have spider guts touch her lips. The revolting taste forced her to sit up, but Millwright was so far away. Surely, Percy would see the danger.

Percy's eyes were closed. He looked like he was on another planet.

"Stop," Ellis urged him, but her voice was barely a whisper.

Standing was like swimming in jam, but she made herself move. She focused on the soles of her boots, which squished in spider guts as she put one foot in front of the other.

Millwright was moving faster than she was. Maybe he could resist his brother's powers. Ellis would not make it.

She scanned her surroundings for a weapon. A DRI soldier at her feet, impaled through the stomach by a spider leg, cradled a gun in his arms like a baby.

"Excuse me." Ellis calmly pried his fingers off the gun.

A breath of air-conditioned air kissed her face, and Ellis savored it before remembering that she had to stop Millwright. She raised the rifle and pointed it at Millwright's cheerful coat. She had no intention of shooting to disable him.

She pulled the trigger, but Millwright kept moving. It took Ellis a moment to realize that she had heard no

MARTHA CARR & MICHAEL ANDERLE

gunshot. She lazily examined the weapon. It was out of ammo.

Inches from Percy, Malcolm raised Welton's dagger. What a shame to have something like that happen on such a nice day.

Claire Burton plunged a dark elf dagger between Malcolm Millwright's shoulder blades. His strangled gasp was covered by Percy's song as he slumped to the floor.

Percy stopped singing, and the spiders stirred. Connor appeared and pressed a bow into her hands. She raised it, only to be interrupted by Percy calling, "Wait!"

The command held the same unconscious compulsion as his song had. Ellis could not have fired if she had wanted to. *Percy, what are you doing?*

Spindly legs twitched and talons clicked as the spiders skittered back into the open vents. After the last glittering eyes disappeared, Percy swayed, then lost his footing. He slid off Flower's strong back onto the floor.

Finally able to move, Ellis caught him before he hit the concrete. His face was gray.

CHAPTER TWENTY-THREE

Percy stared. "My brother's dead."

Millwright lay motionless on the floor. His pant leg had ridden up, exposing his ankle, which was blotchy from the cobra's venom. Claire touched two fingers to his neck, then met Ellis' gaze and shook her head.

Ellis swallowed. "Yes. I'm sorry."

Percy drew several long breaths, then slung an arm over Flower's shoulders and pulled himself upright. "You gotta get outta here. The spiders won't stay calm forever. Mal's manipulations... They stick in your head."

"It's hard to feel sorry for them," Ellis muttered.

He smiled. "Now, now. Spiders make their way through the world just like us."

Ellis glanced at the soldier a spider had stabbed through the gut. Claire and Connor crouched beside him, administering first aid, but his agonized whimpers suggested he disagreed with Percy's claims.

Arden Chan picked toward them through the chaos. She was wearing her heels again due to the disgusting state of the floor. Her face was colorless but determined. She had not lost her cool during the fight. Ellis' respect for the woman grew.

"We should leave," she announced.

Claire looked up from tending the soldier. "We can go up through the social club. The owner's a friend. Well, she knows we exist."

Connor eyed the bloody dagger in Claire's hand. When she noticed, she offered it to him hilt-first. Connor accepted it and carefully wiped the blade, then told Chan, "The drow will leave the way we came. We've rescued our people."

Ellis frowned. "Everyone is badly burned. We'll never make it without being noticed."

Chan spoke up. "I can offer you safe transport. Also, I understand your eagerness to leave, but I wonder if you might consider staying."

Connor's pale fingers tightened around the dagger's hilt. "Why?"

"To talk."

"Your people claimed the drow couldn't speak, and now you want to have a conversation.?" His challenge sliced through the politician's smile.

Chan's gaze was drawn to the red dot spreading on Millwright's paisley lab coat. "I make a point of learning from my mistakes, and it's clear that here, the United States government has made serious mistakes. I need a lot more information." She tore her gaze away and looked at Claire. "If you talk, I might be able to offer you immunity from prosecution."

"She imprisoned and tortured my people," Connor

protested. "She tricked her daughter into providing access to the drow homestead, and unlike some, she knew *precisely* who she was hurting."

"Your *daughter!*" Chan exclaimed.

Connor clamped his mouth shut and growled. Claire cowered from the blaze in his eyes. Ellis guessed he had not intended to reveal that. *I guess I can't* Parent Trap *these two.*

Chan eyed Ellis with new interest. "We have a *great* deal to discuss," she murmured.

Percy interrupted them, strain evident on his face. "As much as I endorse respectful communication, I'm having a *devil* of a time holding these spiders back, so if you could move this circus elsewhere, I would be *greatly* relieved."

An uninjured soldier hoisted his automatic rifle to his hip, and Mirelle nocked an arrow and trained it on the gap between his chest plate and helmet.

Ellis tensed. She was so exhausted that she was about to melt into the floor, but she would fight if she had to.

"What do you want us to do, Doc?" the soldier asked. His gaze was locked on Mirelle.

"Stand down!" Claire barked.

Connor nodded at Mirelle, and the other drow lowered her bow. "There's been enough bloodshed."

Chan gave a sigh of relief. "Now that we're on the same page, let's all go find a nice, quiet place to sit...and some coffee."

Ellis perked up. Maybe she and the senator *would* get along.

The tension peaked several times during the exodus from the facility. In the end, no one dropped their weapons, but no one used them. With Millwright dead, the remaining DRI soldiers deferred to Claire. Connor allowed her free rein but stayed close.

Now they were packed like tinned fish into the hall of Sub-basement Two. Ellis had feared how her father would react to learning she had been growing drow mushroom strains outside the homestead, but he seemed unwilling to add another straw to his back. He thanked her for the rust-caps and administered them to those in the worst shape.

They set human guards near the elevator and stairs, and Senator Chan took the elevator up to speak to Amelia. Ellis was unsurprised to learn that the two knew each other. She *had* wondered how the organization wound up in the Bromeliad's basement. They had been close together for so long and had never realized it.

Ellis marched over to her parents. Emotions still roiled in her heart when she saw them together. "How much does Amelia know about the DRI?"

Claire shrugged. "It's good to have a back door. We use it with official visitors like the senator. We haven't had to muscle our way into favor for a while, but sometimes people need a cover."

She touched a mushroom and pursed her lips. "She shouldn't have started this grow-op without letting us know, and she should have told me you were involved."

Ellis decided she would let Claire and Amelia work that out. Then she thought about Landon for the millionth time. They had left him in the medical facilities with Trissa and Jorel.

A guard approached. "A man named Hector is in the lobby. He wants to talk to you."

Ellis bounded up the stairs and through the door into the lobby. She found Hector looking relaxed in dark eggplant-colored pants and a tight black T-shirt.

She grinned, but he looked horrified. "Oh, my God, Ellis! What happened? Should I call a doctor?" His nose wrinkled. "What is that *smell?*"

Hector snapped his mouth shut when he realized it came from *her.* Ellis caught a glimpse of herself in the lobby doors and understood his alarm. She was covered in blood and spider guts, plus plenty of rock dust.

"I'm fine," she claimed.

"No, you're not!"

She did not have the energy to argue, which meant he had a point. She made a face. "You can help me by rounding up some folding chairs and going on a coffee run."

Hector's eyebrows shot up. "I was thinking more along the lines of calling in the National Guard."

"No!" Her exclamation startled Hector so badly that he backed away, and she awkwardly realized he had been joking. "Just kidding," she weakly offered.

He stared at the black goo on her shirt. "Coffee, huh?"

Ellis attempted an encouraging smile. "Yes?"

Hector shook his head and muttered, "Coffee it is."

"And chairs, please!"

Thirty minutes later, the chairs arrived, along with a drink caddy containing multiple decadent blended coffees and cold brews. Ellis was tempted to claim it all but settled for a cup filled to the brim with coffee, caramel, and whipped cream.

She put the rest out for the others. As she did so, she spied a foil-wrapped burrito with a sticky note on top.

I didn't have time to make soup, but here is a chicken burrito. - H.

Ellis smiled, then flushed when she noticed Charlie watching. They still needed to talk.

After she finished her coffee, Ellis ate half the burrito and gave the rest to her dad.

Connor gaped at it. "I haven't had a burrito in two decades."

"I'm sure the muscle memory will come back to you," Ellis told him. He was too busy stuffing his face to respond.

When they were sufficiently caffeinated and somewhat rested, Ellis sat in a circle with Senator Chan, her parents, Charlie, and Liza.

Chan rested her chin on one hand and glibly stated, "This is the most unusual committee I've ever been part of." How was the woman so composed? Maybe a basement full of magical murderous enemies was peanuts compared to the mudslinging in DC. "Are your people recovering?" she asked Connor.

"I'm not sure," her father responded honestly. His mouth was set in a tight line. Before the meeting, Ellis had gone back down to see Landon. He still would not speak, although Trissa had convinced him to drink the rustcap broth.

Chan nodded, then turned to Claire. "Let me be clear that I've invited you as a courtesy. I assure you that the DRI will not continue in its current form."

The weight lifted from Ellis' shoulders. "Can you guarantee that?"

Chan smiled. "Few people are allowed to make decisions about top-secret research institutes. I'm confident that my recommendation will stand."

Based on her impression of Arden Chan, Ellis was equally confident. "Will you have to worry about former DRI soldiers talking to the media?" she inquired.

Chan considered the question. "I don't think so. Not any more than before, anyway. I'll ensure that the soldiers' exit interviews are...assertive."

"What about justice?" Connor interjected.

Chan raised an eyebrow. "In what sense?"

"If a drow committed the types of crimes the DRI has committed, they would be brought before a council of elders. Consequences would range from detention to hard labor to, in extreme circumstances, dissolution."

He stopped speaking, but his expression was clear. The DRI's actions toward the captive drow counted as "extreme circumstances."

Chan laid her hands in her lap, palms up. "Regular courts are out of the question."

"Why?"

"Court cases are public record, and your existence is a state secret."

"That's not up to you to decide," Connor pointed out.

Ellis jerked upright. "You can't be suggesting that we publicize our existence."

Connor pursed his lips. "I'm not, but that is up to *us*, not the United States government."

"While *I* agree, I'm not sure everyone in Washington

will see it the same way," Chan countered. "My colleagues who receive campaign funding from defense contractors would be particularly disinclined. No decent person would want to start a war on US soil, but—"

Ellis cut her off. "'War?' What do you mean, a *war*?"

Chan grimaced. "War is profitable, especially for those who would be eager to label you enemy combatants."

"We will not go to war," Connor firmly stated. "We are going home."

"If you want me to arrest someone, just point," Charlie Morrissey interjected, and Ellis smiled. "I've lost count of the number of infractions that would be of interest to the LAPD and the FBI. Hell, I'll call the UN. Say the word, and this place will be crawling with alphabet soup."

"Assuming you wouldn't be arrested for kidnapping a senator," Chan retorted.

Charlie shrugged. "I'll take my licks. Some things are more important than my career."

Ellis sighed. "No, my dad's right. We just want to go home."

Chan looked relieved. "I'm glad to hear it." She paused, then added, "My chief of staff would kill me for this, but for what it's worth, please accept my personal apology."

Connor nodded. "Thank you."

She frowned. "As to the question of justice, as I said, conventional courts are not an option. That leaves the military courts, which might not take issue with Dr. Burton's conduct."

"She tortured people," Ellis insisted.

Connor's jaw tightened. "She tortured *our* people. Is that what you're saying?"

Color rose in Chan's cheeks. "I don't agree, but they might see it that way. That route also risks further military exposure."

Her tone had lightened, but her gaze was serious. "On the other hand, if Dr. Burton chose to confess to, say, embezzlement of government funds, military custody might keep her safe from invisible magical enemies."

Ellis was reasonably certain that Chan was inferring the drow were capable of avenging themselves on Claire unless she was locked up. "Nothing like that would happen!" she protested, but a glance around the circle told her she was the only one who believed it.

Claire shook her head. "I won't confess to embezzlement. My sins lie elsewhere."

Ellis sighed. You had to pick your battles. "What will you do with the basement?"

Chan raised an eyebrow. "What were *you* planning on doing? Humor me."

"I planned to collapse the facility," Connor admitted.

Claire gaped at him, as did Ellis, although it no longer mattered. They did not have the power for that kind of spellwork since so many had been burned by lightsilk.

Arden half-shrugged. "I suppose we'll brick it up. Sell the office chairs, archive the documents, and so forth. That kind of facilities work isn't in my purview."

A soft voice spoke up. "Lucky for you, I have an excellent facilities manager."

Amelia insouciantly regarded the surprised faces. The Bromeliad's owner did not blink at Connor's purple face among the others in the circle.

Chan nodded politely. "Hello, Amelia. Stand down, boys."

Amelia eyed the two black-clad guards who had stepped up behind her. They just as quickly stepped away.

"You knew about the drow!" Ellis accused.

Amelia raised an eyebrow until Chan clarified, "She means the MECs."

Ellis opened her mouth to protest, but Amelia spoke first. "Ah, yes. There was an incident several years back. I encountered a chromatically aberrant young man who had escaped and signed the State Secrets Act, blah blah blah." She dismissively waved a hand.

The spore of an idea sprouted in Ellis' mind. "It would be a shame to lose the real estate."

Amelia's smile was smug. "Oh?"

"Maybe there's a middle ground between full disclosure and complete isolation."

"What are you suggesting?" Cautious interest appeared on Chan's face.

"What if the drow established an outpost in Los Angeles?" Ellis suggested. "A place where we could interact with the human world, and where…where we could live if our apartment complexes were burned down by the DRI."

Claire averted her gaze, but Connor looked at Ellis. "You're not coming home?" His tone was wounded.

Ellis grimaced. "I'm making my own home, Dad. I'll come see you and Landon, but—"

Amelia interjected, her ever-present smile regaining its hungry edge, "What a lovely idea. We could use the DRI's equipment to turn your little mushroom-growing operation into a *big* mushroom-growing operation. We would share vital mycological research with the US military, of course. Wouldn't we, Ellis?"

Her voice wrapped around Ellis' mind and squeezed, and her hand rested lightly on Ellis' shoulder. Ellis was uncomfortably reminded of Percy's siren song.

"Um, yeah." She would decide whether she meant it later.

Chan nodded. "I might be able to find you funding. Call it...I don't know, a transition program. If Dr. Burton was willing to stay on—"

"No!" Connor snapped as Ellis exclaimed, "Yes!" Despite everything, she was not ready to give up on her mother.

Chan cleared her throat and continued. "*If* Dr. Burton was willing to stay on as part of the *archival process*, we could keep the Department of Defense out of your business long enough for you to spin up your new projects. To be honest, it feels like the least I can do."

Claire turned a hopeful gaze on Ellis. "What do you say?"

"I guess I'm back to toiling in the mushroom caverns," Ellis replied.

Chan chuckled. "You're an interesting diplomat. Now, an important part of diplomacy is the exchange of information and resources..."

Ellis narrowed her eyes. "What are you saying?"

"Given the circumstances, I see no point in dancing around the issue. If I let you set up an outpost in the basement, a time might come when the United States government calls on you for help with tasks suited to your particular skills. I expect any such call to be answered."

Ellis raised an eyebrow. "You scratch my back, I scratch yours?"

"Precisely."

Ellis pursed her lips, then met her father's gaze. Connor looked unconvinced for a moment, then shrugged. It was up to her.

She nodded. "All right, Senator. You have a deal."

Chan smiled. "In that case, I look forward to working together."

Excitement surged through Ellis as they shook hands. She had a mother and a new job that might genuinely help the drow, and she and her father had finally been honest with one another. What could possibly come next?

THE STORY CONTINUES

The story continues with The Chronicles of Shadow Bourne book five, coming soon to Amazon and Kindle Unlimited.

Get sneak peeks, exclusive giveaways, behind the scenes content, and more. PLUS you'll be notified of special **one day only fan pricing** on new releases.

Sign up today to get free stories.

Visit: https://marthacarr.com/read-free-stories/

AUTHOR NOTES - MARTHA CARR

WRITTEN MARCH 8, 2024

The garden is under way again. If you're new to these author notes, I have a pretty standard suburban home with a nice backyard. Back in 2020 (remember that year?), I finally set out on a dream of mine. I got help designing a garden that stretches half of the front yard, because that's all the HOA will let me in the front, down both sides with peach and fig trees and other plants, and all the way across the back. There are even raised beds for vegetables and herbs.

There's a tall elm in the middle in the back that had to be hoisted to get it back there. Shade in Texas. It can't be beat.

Everyone's favorite is the bench with a metal arch built over it that is now covered in crossvine blooming at the moment with pale peach flowers shaped like trumpets. The arch is covered in them, and more than one engaged couple has had their picture taken there. My inspiration was the live willow arches of England. That was not possible here in Texas so a compromise was discovered. A good lesson with gardening. You may not get what you want a lot of the time, but if you can lean into what is there you will probably get a pleasant surprise.

Kind of a great life lesson that helps with books too.

My goal with the garden was to provide food, water, and shelter to any living thing. Yes, that includes the mice who show up occasionally and live in the compost box or the wasps, which are also pollinators. There are lizards everywhere and songbirds and worms and roly polies and butterflies and bees and more. All good signs of a healthy dirt, which is the foundation of everything else.

A young, male feral pig even found his way into the front garden this past summer during the long, dry heat, and helped me dig up part of the garden, free of charge. I totally got it. Cool, wet dirt and a few grubs to munch on must have felt like heaven. We parted on fairly good terms. After the third visit and the relocation of part of my sprinkler system I laid down some cayenne powder – twice. He moved back in with his herd after that who thankfully never found their way over to my place.

The garden has been in full swing for three years now. I had to wait a year for the design because all of us had the same thought during quarantine about doing something better with the yard we were staring at day after day.

In that time, I've dealt with frost, and extended drought, and sudden and lengthy rains and thunderstorms that made everything stand up, and then spring. Wonderful spring when everything starts to come back at last. Wildflowers return on their own and pop up in unexpected places thanks to the birds. Every year it feels like they help with some of the design and somehow it always fits seamlessly.

But that was kind of my point as well. I wanted the garden to feel natural and not completely by design.

It's also my happy place and when I'm out in the garden working, covered in sunscreen, I forget about everything. My brain turns off and I am digging my hands in the dirt, looking for critters and feeling the breeze against my skin. Heaven.

To those of you that are still waiting for spring, it's coming! Can you feel the anticipation? Maybe that's just a gardener's joy. Off to write, maybe garden a little at the end of the day now that the sunshine is lasting longer. More adventures to follow.

AUTHOR NOTES - MICHAEL ANDERLE

WRITTEN MARCH 12, 2024

Thank you so much for reading our stories to the end, and now, reading these author notes in the back.

Occasionally, I talk about where I am at (London for the London Book Fair at the moment—it's dreadfully cold and raining). Sometimes, I talk about my family (it's all good, thanks for asking), and now I'm going to talk about why I like writing Drow-type characters.

There's something inherently magnetic about these dark elves that continue to draw me in, time and time again, and here are four of my main top reasons I go back to the Drow:

Drizzt: The Inspiration

Let's start with the most iconic Drow of all, Drizzt Do'Urden. If you haven't read his story, here is the first book that has Drizzt that got me hooked: https://en.wikipedia.org/wiki/The_Halfling% 27s_Gem.

Drizzt is the epitome of a character who defies the

odds, challenges stereotypes, and carves his own path—an individual in a society known for malice and deceit.

His badassery is not just in his combat prowess but in his moral courage to stand against the darkness from which he came.

He is a *major* reason for my love affair with the Drow archetype; he's the outcast who became a hero, the antithesis of his kin, and a character that resonates with anyone who's ever felt different. In short, he is a badass with a heart of gold.

Rebelling Against the Norm

Drow don't just walk the path less traveled—they blaze it. They're the rebels of the elfin world, unburdened by the expectations of their surface-dwelling cousins, those tree-huggers we know as elves. This sense of rebellion, this freedom to be unabashedly badass, is incredibly appealing to me as a creator. It's the ultimate form of self-expression, and isn't that what we all seek in some form or another?

Fashionably Dark

Let's talk clothes—because, let's face it, Drow have style. They embrace the color black like no other, and their outfits reflect their fierce personalities. Since they are often underground, it isn't like there is a lot of color.

As someone who's always preferred the sleek, enigmatic allure of black attire, designing Drow characters and their wardrobes is a particular pleasure. They're the rock stars of the fantasy world, and I'm here for it.

A Writer's Dream

Finally, crafting a Drow character is, for a writer like me, an exercise in creative liberation.

When your starting point is a society of backstabbers -

starting with your closest family members - and, let's be honest, complete jackholes, any Drow with a shred of decency or complexity instantly becomes fascinating.

Drow family stories can make Harry Potter's issues seem trite
Whether it's their defiance, their style, or their potential for profound character development, the Drow hold a special place in my writer's notebook. They're the underdogs, the misfits, and the renegades—and with them as an ingredient in the story?

I find endless inspiration.

So here's to the Drow, to the Drizzts of the world, and to all the characters who dare to be different.

Like Ellis.

May they continue to remind us that even in the darkest of places, there's potential for greatness.

Talk to you in the next story!

Ad Aeternitatem,

Michael Anderle

MORE STORIES with Michael HERE:
https://michael.beehiiv.com/

BOOKS BY MARTHA CARR

Other Series in the Oriceran Universe:

THE LEIRA CHRONICLES
CASE FILES OF AN URBAN WITCH
SOUL STONE MAGE
THE KACY CHRONICLES
MIDWEST MAGIC CHRONICLES
THE FAIRHAVEN CHRONICLES
I FEAR NO EVIL
THE DANIEL CODEX SERIES
SCHOOL OF NECESSARY MAGIC
SCHOOL OF NECESSARY MAGIC: RAINE CAMPBELL
ALISON BROWNSTONE
FEDERAL AGENTS OF MAGIC
SCIONS OF MAGIC
THE UNBELIEVABLE MR. BROWNSTONE
DWARF BOUNTY HUNTER
ACADEMY OF NECESSARY MAGIC
MAGIC CITY CHRONICLES
ROGUE AGENTS OF MAGIC

OTHER BOOKS BY JUDITH BERENS

OTHER BOOKS BY MARTHA CARR

JOIN THE ORICERAN UNIVERSE FAN GROUP ON FACEBOOK!

CONNECT WITH THE AUTHORS

Martha Carr Social

Website: http://www.marthacarr.com

Facebook: https://www.facebook.com/groups/MarthaCarrFans/

Michael Anderle Social

Website: http://lmbpn.com

Email List: https://michael.beehiiv.com/

https://www.facebook.com/LMBPNPublishing

https://twitter.com/MichaelAnderle

https://www.instagram.com/lmbpn_publishing/

https://www.bookbub.com/authors/michael-anderle

Made in the USA
Middletown, DE
13 December 2024

66867094R00139